BATGIRL

TO DARE THE DARKNESS

D0249325

WARNER BROS. PRESENTS

A JOEL SCHUMACHER FILM ARNOLD SCHWARZENEGGER GEORGE CLOONEY CHRIS O'DONNELL UMA THURMAN ALICIA SILVERSTONE "BATMAN & ROBIN" MICHAEL GOUGH PAT HINGLE ELLE MACPHERSON

MUSIC ELLIOT GOLDENTHAL EXECUTIVE BENJAMIN MELNIKER AND MICHAEL E. USLAN BASED UPON CHARACTERS APPEARING CREATED BY BOB KANE PUBLISHED BY DC COMICS WRITTEN BY AKIVA GOLDSMAN PRODUCED BY PETER MACGREGOR-SCOTT

DIRECTED BY JOEL SCHUMACHER

WWW.BATMAN-ROBIN.COM

BATGIRL

TO DARE THE DARKNESS

by Doug Moench

Batman created by Bob Kane

Little, Brown and Company

Boston   New York   Toronto   London

For my family: Winnie, Gil, Pam, Debra, and Derek

First Edition

Library of Congress Cataloging-in-Publication Data

Moench, Doug
   Batgirl : to dare the darkness / by Doug Moench. — 1st ed.
      p.   cm.
   "Batman created by Bob Kane."
   Summary: When the master criminal Black Mask launches the False
Face Society of Gotham, a small army of zombies, Batgirl is on hand
to help Batman and Robin fight them.
   ISBN 0-316-17695-8
   [1. Heroes — Fiction.   2. Adventure and adventurers — Fiction.]
I. Title.
PZ7.M7195Bat   1997
[Fic] — dc21   97-7079

10 9 8 7 6 5 4 3 2 1

COM-MO

Published simultaneously in Canada
by Little, Brown & Company (Canada) Limited

Printed in the United States of America

CHAPTER 1

MYSTERY CHIPS

The edge of the city was a good place to fight crime. The rotting docks and sagging piers of the Gotham wharves formed a bleak bulwark against the black waters of the bay. A mournful foghorn moaned through distant mist. Then the night fell silent, save for unseen splashings against posts and pilings that creaked and groaned and seemed to sigh.

It was a nasty place at night, with the sure sense that anything could happen. The fog-blurred moon hung low and nearly full, but with no hint of magic, no romance. Even the shadows seemed sinister, dirty, and rough, with the grit of black sandpaper.

Crouched in those shadows, behind stacks of off-loaded crates, was a young woman. Her name was Barbara Wilson, but that was not who she was now, not at night. Caped and clad in a tight dark costume designed to strike fear in the hearts of criminals, she was an avenging creature of the night. She was Batgirl, or at least she hoped she was. Still a rookie in this hero game, she knew she had to perform like a veteran. There was no room for mistakes in life-or-death situations. Her partners were waiting nearby, depending on her.

Smugglers were coming, and they were intent on feeding the city their cargo, its nature unknown but illicit. The police informant's tip said they were rough men who would rather fight than surrender. Just thinking about it made her heart begin to pound. Crime was coming, but suddenly she did not feel like a creature of the night. She felt like a frightened child, and hated herself for it. The night had begun so well. Donning her dark costume, she had swelled with confidence, eager to fight the good fight and ready to conquer all comers. But now . . .

She caught her breath, suddenly aware of the hum of an engine, startlingly clear as it carried across the water. It grew louder, until the dark shape of a small ship loomed from the fog. No running lights. This was a secret docking.

The engine coughed and died. Silently, the ship scudded the last fifty yards before gently bumping the dock. Barbara realized she was still holding her breath. She let it out slowly, lips parted, careful to make no sound.

She peered around the edge of a crate. A large man jumped from ship's prow to wharf's planks with a loud thump. A rope was tossed to him. He wrapped it around a

mooring cleat, then moved down the wharf to the rear of the ship and did the same with a second tossed rope. The vessel was secured.

Barbara's heart pounded harder. *No,* she thought, *it's Batgirl's heart, and that heart must be strong and fierce and always under control.* She stared across the dark waters past the ship, focusing on the moon, concentrating on its brightness. She let it fill her eyes and her mind, using its light to center her soul and calm her emotions. It was so much easier when the action exploded without warning, when there was nothing to do but react. This waiting game was different. It was, in fact, excruciating. There was too much suspense, too much time to think.

Gruff voices muttered from the ship, the words impossible to make out. A plank was lowered to the dock. Other men clumped down the plank, each carrying a crate. Two of them, four, six . . . and more still to come.

This was it, the point of no return. Tensing every muscle in her body, Barbara focused and set her mind, *willing* her heart to slow its beat.

Then she surged from her cover and broke into a full sprint, determined to be first into the fray.

But she was already too late. A dark shape was dropping from the arm of a loading crane, its cape snapping and fluttering like the wings of a giant bat. The figure landed facing the stunned smugglers. It was the Batman, a *true* creature of the night, and his voice grated like flint on tombstone: "Drop the crates and stand back with your hands on your heads."

The smugglers stood like statues fused to the dock. Even Barbara, who had known where Batman was stationed, was stopped in her tracks by the effect of his entrance. *Talk about striking fear . . .*

One crate crashed to the dock, followed by the others. The smugglers were dropping them as ordered, but their hands were not going slowly to their heads. They had fight or flight in mind, maybe both, but not surrender. Then there was a confusion of quick movement and something glinted in the moonlight. A gun.

Barbara grabbed at her belt, reaching for a Batarang, but again she was too late. Batman's hand had already whipped from the folds of his cloak. His Batarang smacked the gun even as it discharged, and the blast was forced harmlessly high with not a second to spare.

No doubt about it, Barbara thought, *I've still got a lot to learn.*

Then Robin, Batman's other partner, was swooping into view, a blur of red, green, and gold swinging on a clinking chain, kicking away a second gun Barbara hadn't even noticed. Guns were always first priority, she knew. Avoid them or eliminate them. It was Batman's cardinal rule, drummed into her head every day during training. Their costumes were reinforced with bulletproof Kevlar, but a point-blank shot could still do damage. Batman despised guns, a hatred tracing to the murder of his parents. Indeed, it was that traumatic event which had turned Bruce Wayne into the Batman.

He was a dark fury now, doing battle with five of the smugglers, and even at those odds it was no contest. Robin had dropped from his chain onto two other criminals, leaving one unaccounted for on the dock and maybe more still aboard the ship.

Barbara scanned the melee and spied the first smuggler kneeling over the aft mooring cleat, unwinding the rope in a bid to escape. She moved swiftly in his direction. He sensed her rush, rising and turning to meet it, but Barbara's fist smashed into his face before he fully knew what was coming.

The man staggered back, and Barbara clutched her fist as pain shot up her arm. Even though she had felt the sting before, it still shocked her. But it also made the situation real. She shook off the pain, knowing that a threshold had been instantly crossed, that the warrior spirit of Batgirl was claiming her heart.

With her other hand, she slashed a chop to the dazed man's neck and vaulted aboard the ship even as he fell.

The ship swayed gently under her feet. She adjusted her balance, finding the rhythm of the bay's lapping swells.

This was better now. The pain in her hand had faded and her blood was high. The action had begun and there was no room for fear, no place for Barbara Wilson. She was Batgirl now, and she felt at one with the night. She was a predator, preying on evil.

Holding perfectly still, every sense attuned, Batgirl peered into the ship's gloom and shadows. Batman and Robin were still battling on the dock, but she knew there might be more men here on the ship. Were they hiding? And if so, where?

She heard a slight sound and glimpsed movement beyond the ship's housing, up on the forward deck. It seemed like a single figure, but she couldn't be certain. Silently, she crept along the ship's rail, past the housing.

There he was, not moving, masquerading as a shadow, hoping she wouldn't notice his human shape, hoping she would venture close enough for him to strike without warning.

Batgirl stopped and spoke to the shadow: "Give it up. Now!"

The shadow moved, becoming a large, rough man with less than a full set of teeth displayed in a sneer. He flicked his fingers at his chest and laughed with a growl. "Just a *girl* — and you think you can take *me?* Come on, girlie — let's dance!"

Batgirl's eyes glittered, her lips forming a mirthless

smile. She started to move forward, but froze as a second smuggler stepped from the gloom, a long boathook extending from his gnarled hands. Then there were sounds from the rear — two more men coming from below deck, emerging from the ship's housing, both armed with clubs.

Batgirl bent her knees into a slight crouch, keeping her weight centered but light on the balls of her feet. She slipped a Batarang from her belt and held it loosely, ready to snap it like a truncheon.

The unarmed smuggler spoke: "How eager are you *now,* girlie?"

"My dance card's still open, handsome. But since I seem to be surrounded at all four corners . . . let's make it a *square* dance."

She flicked her eyes from one smuggler to the next, then back again, searching for the first lunge. But as one, all four started closing in. Slowly . . .

Something hurtled over the heads of two of the smugglers, and suddenly Robin was at Batgirl's side. He flashed a lopsided grin, set his back to hers, and said, "Need some help?"

"Not really," she bluffed. "There's only four of them — and just three are armed."

"No need to get greedy," said Robin. "That still leaves two for each of us."

Abruptly, the smugglers rushed inward. Batgirl side-stepped the unarmed man and angled a high kick to meet the downward slash of the boathook. It split in half across the bottom of her boot.

Robin leaped high, scissoring his legs outward to kick the chins of both club-wielders at the same time.

Batgirl spun away to face the unarmed thug, snapping her Batarang to the back of his neck. She hit the nerve center perfectly and the man went down as deadweight, his sneer wiped slack even before his face hit the deck.

"Lost a few more teeth, did we?" said Batgirl.

She turned back to the man with the broken boathook just as he swung the splintered remnant of his stick. Her hands shot out, caught the pole with a sharp smack, and stopped it cold. Then she yanked hard, jerking the man off-balance and right into a kick to his gut. He doubled over as the breath left his body. Then he grunted and sat down hard, staring up at Batgirl. His eyes glazed over and slowly closed, then he pitched over sideways.

Batgirl cast the broken pole away and turned to look back over her shoulder. The two club-wielders were also sprawled on the deck. Robin was making a show of dusting his gloved hands, a huge grin beaming below his domino mask. Batgirl grinned back at him, and they slapped high-fives.

"*Ahar,* me mateys!" said Robin in the raspy voice of a movie pirate. "Methinks the booty be ours."

Flushed with triumph, Batgirl joined in: "And these four swabs never even walked the plank."

Robin punched her shoulder and she punched his right back. They clapped arms around each other and laughed.

The moonlight was abruptly eclipsed, casting them into deep shadow. Their laughter died as they looked up to see a cloaked figure standing atop the ship's housing, looming over them like a giant. The Batman. He was staring down at them. But was he glowering? It was impossible to tell; he was all darkness, a long cape with tall sharp ears.

The eerie wail of sirens ripped the night. Batgirl and Robin turned to see the spinning lights of marked and unmarked police cars screeching onto the dock. From above and behind them, a deep voice intoned: "It's not a *game*."

They turned back. There was the moon again. Batman was gone.

Police Commissioner James Gordon stepped from his unmarked car onto the warped planks of the dock. He removed his hat to run a hand through silver hair. He looked haggard and haunted, showing the effects of too many long nights in a city where every night is long.

Batman stepped from the shadows. "Good work," the Commissioner said, "as usual."

The Batman nodded but said nothing.

Commissioner Gordon turned to Robin. "You too, son."

"Any time, Commish."

Gordon then turned to his uniformed police officers. They were using crowbars to open the smugglers' crates.

Not a word to me, thought Batgirl. *He didn't even look in my direction.* True, she was hanging back, keeping her distance ever since Batman's reprimand, but still . . . did Commissioner Gordon think she was nothing more than decoration? Some kind of team mascot? The slight truly stung, far more than that first punch. *I held my own during this operation — and then some. If he can't see —*

"Vegetables, Commissioner." It was one of the police officers, hunched over an opened crate. "Nothing but vegetables."

Gordon frowned. "Vegetables?"

"Lettuce." The officer shrugged. "Cabbage. Stuff like that."

Now Gordon was actually irritated. "No one smuggles *lettuce.*"

Batman upended a crate, bouncing heads of cabbage across the dock. His gauntleted hand probed inside the empty crate. "False bottom." He dashed the crate to the dock. The bottom shattered, and out skittered dozens of small identical items. They looked like square buttons glittering in the moonlight.

Batman slowly turned one of them between thumb and

forefinger, catching the dim light to examine it from every angle. "Silicon chips," he announced. "Miniature electronic circuits."

Gordon stepped forward for a closer look. "They're smuggling stolen computer parts?"

"I don't think so, Commissioner. These chips are like none I've ever seen. Extremely unusual design. I think they're custom-made."

"But for what?" Gordon was genuinely puzzled. "Our informant claimed these smugglers have been making monthly runs into Gotham. What's so valuable about these chips? What are they?"

"Until I find out, Commissioner, they're *nothing*."

Batman slipped several of them into a container on his Utility Belt. Then he looked up, into the dark distance, his masked face grim. "Nothing but . . . mystery chips."

CHAPTER 2
HIDDEN FACES

The Dark Side of the Moon nightclub had been abandoned when the neighborhood turned bad. Its overlaid facade of bolted boards, plywood panels, and sprayed graffiti served to disguise its true face — one of many underworld hideouts tucked into the dark corners of Gotham. Where celebrants had once laughed and dined and danced, criminals now gathered.

In a back room, one such criminal sat hunched over a long workbench. His face was hidden by a Chinese dragon mask. On the bench before him lay a row of nine other masks, most of them tribal, some of them garish, all of them bizarre. The dragon-faced man turned the first mask over, exposing a small slot in the forehead area of its inner surface.

Then the crime boss known as Black Mask entered the room. He wore a brimmed hat, black gloves, and a dark double-breasted suit out of an old gangster movie. None of the criminals who served him had ever seen his face — just his polished ebony mask, sinister and not quite human. When he spoke, his words were deeply muffled. "You're preparing for the nine new members?"

The dragon-masked man at the bench did not turn from his methodical work, yet replied immediately and in tones of total obedience: "Yes, Black Mask." As he had done with the first of the nine masks, he now inserted something into the slot within the second. "Everything will be ready for the initiation ceremony, but we *are* running low for future recruits."

Black Mask grunted hollowly. "Don't worry. A fresh shipment arrived tonight. Enough to build a small army."

A third man, wearing the hawk-head mask of the Egyptian god Horus, entered the room. "Trouble on the docks, Black Mask."

"What kind of trouble?"

The hawk-faced man shifted his weight, seeming nervous. "We . . . we drove down," he said, "to pick up the shipment like you ordered . . ."

"And you took it over to the warehouse?"

"Uh . . . no, not exactly. We . . . uh . . ."

"Spit it out!" Black Mask commanded.

"Well . . . we stopped when we saw all these lights. Cop cars, all over the dock, so we . . . we turned around and came back."

Black Mask jerked his head and stared off at nothing. When he finally spoke, his voice was murderous. "Gordon," he said. "And he'll pay. His whole *city* will pay."

Then he shoved Horus aside and stalked out of the room.

At the workbench, the Chinese dragon inserted a small square button into the inner surface of the ninth mask. His work done, he stopped and sat utterly still. His mask showed no emotion, nor did it hide any. The dragon simply awaited further orders. As did the god Horus.

Three gleaming vehicles roared through a jagged tunnel of stalactites and stalagmites, coming to a halt in the main area of the Batcave, which sprawled beneath Wayne Manor. Robin leaped off his Redbird motorcycle, moving toward the Batmobile even as Batman emerged. Batgirl watched, still astride her sleek Batblade cycle, as Batman accepted Robin's presence without objection. The two moved off toward the cave's crime-lab area, side by side, as if partnered since birth. Even their strides were in sync, swift and long, although Robin had to strain a bit to keep up.

Batgirl dismounted and followed at a distance, feeling like an unnecessary third wheel. As the newcomer to this team, she wondered if she would *ever* find her place in the tight bond between Batman and Robin.

Still keeping her distance, Batgirl nevertheless watched with keen interest as Batman shifted to his intense detective mode. He analyzed the mystery chips under microscope and spectroscope, in black light and red. He immersed them in various chemical solutions and checked them again. He compared them against a full range of other, conventional silicon chips. Through it all, he said nothing.

Robin had wandered off a short distance to the parallel bars, where he was working through a routine of twists and flips, honing his acrobatic abilities. As Dick Grayson, a member of the Flying Graysons circus act, he had been a world-class aerialist even before meeting Batman. Now, knowing that his mentor might well be absorbed for hours, he saw no reason not to sharpen his skills even further.

But Batgirl watched the analysis with rapt attention. She was still in her dark outfit but had long since removed her mask. Gradually, as the exultation of the battle on the docks ebbed, she found herself becoming Barbara Wilson again. And as a young woman who would major in computer studies in the fall, she was particularly fascinated by Batman's work.

Finally, the Darknight Detective linked three circuit boards in sequence, soldered one of the mystery chips into the makeshift electronic maze, and connected the whole to an amplifier.

Dick rejoined them in street clothes, scruffing his wet hair with a towel, just as Batman flipped a switch on the amplifier. Test tubes vibrated and clinked in their tray on a nearby lab table. Barbara felt a dull ache in her head, a rhythmic pulsing that was distinctly unpleasant, even disturbing.

Dick actually clutched the towel on his head and yelped.

Batman flicked the switch off.

Dick smacked the side of his head like a swimmer trying to jolt water from his ear. "What was *that?*"

"I haven't fully cracked the mystery," Batman said, "but I have determined that these chips are capable of producing ELF waves."

"Elf waves," Dick repeated. "For midget surfers?"

The Batman was not amused. "ELF stands for extremely low frequency waves."

"I knew that." Dick grinned, even though he hadn't known it at all. "Stereo or surround-sound components? Chips for driving subwoofers?"

Barbara stepped forward. "Subwoofers produce bass tones meant to be heard," she said. "I felt something, but I didn't really hear anything."

"None of us did," Batman said. "ELF waves resonate far too low for the range of normal human hearing."

"What about bat ears?" Dick asked. "Too low for them too?"

Batman ignored him, staring down at the implanted mystery chip. "Low enough, in fact, to be harmful to the human brain."

Then he pulled off his cowl. It was almost dawn, and Batman was done for the night. It was time for Bruce Wayne to begin his day as the chief executive of Wayne Enterprises.

The Dark Side of the Moon's main area was a vast room, dim and nearly empty. A number of masked guards were stationed near the cracked and stained walls, all facing inward. Black Mask himself stood atop a table in the center of the room. Suspended from the ceiling above him was a large disco ball caked with years of dust. Below him were the nine new recruits, each holding a mask in his hands. They looked up at him, ready for initiation into the False Face Society of Gotham.

Black Mask raised a gloved hand to signal the start of the ceremony. "You are about to experience a secret power," he said, "and it is the Power of the Mask."

The nine recruits shifted uneasily, exchanging glances, not knowing whether they should shudder or laugh.

Black Mask continued, his muffled voice growing louder, as if reciting an incantation of increasing potency: "Know that the mask destroys one identity while creating another! Know that the mask reshapes and remakes its wearer, altering the former personality and eliminating all inhibitions! It disguises the wearer even as it intimidates the wearer's victim! Any deed becomes possible behind a mask, and that is just a part of the Power!"

Then he stopped to let the speech sink in, and to observe its effect.

One man from out of town, a car thief holding the mask of a Sumerian demon, muttered softly from the side of his mouth, "Is this gink kiddin' with all the mask blather? It's a joke."

The man next to him, a homegrown arsonist holding the inlaid mask of a Mayan priest, hissed back, "Quiet. This 'gink' is already the biggest crime boss in town, and his gang's the place to be in Gotham. The masks are weird, maybe, but they make sense — unless you wanna be identified by some witness after a job."

Black Mask was amused by the furiously whispered exchange. He had not made out the actual words, but he could guess the gist of them. Skepticism was nothing new among recruits. They all thought he was crazy, at first. It was time, now, to initiate these nine into the same blind belief and obedience that governed his veteran followers. "I see some of you still have doubts," he intoned loudly. "But the Power of the Mask is real, and you hold the proof of it in your hands. Don the masks! Become the Power they hold! Become new entities!"

Several of the nine obeyed at once, eager to join this mysterious man's gang, desperate to become rich without working. The others lifted their masks more hesitantly, feeling ridiculous. The Sumerian demon was the last mask put in place.

Finally, when all nine had succumbed to greed and stood before him with their faces covered, Black Mask was satisfied. He reached a gloved finger to a small button concealed in the temple area of his own mask. "And now," he said, "feel the Power of the Mask."

He pressed the button.

There was no audible sound, but the nine initiates clutched their heads and spasmed violently. Several made guttural noises of pain.

But it was all over within seconds, whereupon the nine men stood still, almost at attention, much like the perimeter guards. Docile but waiting.

The mind behind the Sumerian demon mask no longer thought it was a joke. Indeed, for as long as he wore his activated mask, or merely remained within its range, he would no longer think or say or do anything — except whatever was commanded by Black Mask.

The Power of the Mask *was* a very real phenomenon,

but all the power emanated from a single mask, the one that was capable of transmitting but not receiving extremely low frequency waves, the one that was very carefully insulated against ELF waves. It was a dark mask carved from the lid of an ebony coffin, and supposedly imbued with all the power of death. And so, atop a table in vast gloom, under a faintly glittering ball of mirrors, Black Mask stood supreme above his brain-dead followers.

His False Face Society of Gotham was now a small but growing army of zombie puppets, all emotion blanked from their hidden faces.

CHAPTER 3
FALLEN MASKS

The next night, a black bat encircled by bright light wavered in the dark Gotham sky. The movement of low clouds seemed to give the bat life, but it was just an emblem, a signal sent on a strong shaft of light from the roof of police headquarters.

At the base of the Bat-Signal beacon, Commissioner Gordon stood facing three dark angels. Even though she was one of the participants, Barbara found the scene entirely unreal. *What am I doing here?* she wondered. *If someone had told me, just a month ago, that I'd be standing in a stiff wind on this high roof, under a giant bat in the sky, dressed like this* . . . She gave up, shaking her strangely masked head.

"Thanks for responding," the Commissioner said — and once again Barbara noticed that he seemed to ignore her. His attention was focused almost solely on Batman, but at least his eyes flicked briefly in Robin's direction. It was a lot more than what came her way, which was nothing.

"Trouble, Commissioner?" Batman asked. "Or news?"

"Maybe both," Gordon replied. "We finally got one of the smugglers to talk. That shipment of . . . of 'mystery chips' . . . it was supposed to be picked up by two men coming from a small electronics factory in South Gotham. I had undercover teams staked out on the docks all night, but no one showed."

"We watched for an hour ourselves," Batman said, "from the shadows. I suspect the pickup men were scared off by your lights."

Gordon grunted, pushing up on the bridge of his eyeglasses. "Anyway," he continued, "the smuggler isn't sure, but he's heard rumors that the electronics factory could be a front for Black Mask."

Batman showed increased interest. "Still no leads on him, Commissioner?"

"Nothing. He's like a ghost. Every time we think we're getting close, he's simply gone."

"He probably keeps a number of hideouts, constantly moving from one to another with no set pattern."

"Makes sense," Gordon said, "plus he could be anyone without his mask. Until we know his face, he's free to move through the city at will. But one thing's for sure: His activities are escalating. More and more crimes committed by his 'False Facers' every night . . ."

Barbara sensed that the Commissioner was building up to something but was reluctant to get to the point.

Evidently Batman sensed the same. "About this electronics factory, Commissioner . . . ?"

Gordon drew a breath, let it out. He looked at Batman, then turned away before speaking. "My men could raid the place," he said, "but I'd need a court order, and at this time of night . . ."

Batman nodded to Robin. "This time of night, Commissioner, is *perfect* for us."

The small factory was dark and silent. Batgirl carefully bridged and snipped both alarm wires leading to the window at which she was stationed. Then she peered inside.

Batman slid down a line from a skylight and dropped to the floor. Remaining in his crouch, he looked this way and that. Shadowy bulks loomed nearly everywhere — boxed audio components stacked on skids — but nothing moved. Finally, Batman signaled to two different windows.

Robin eased his window open and slipped inside.

But as soon as Barbara opened her window, a harsh clangor shattered the night. *The alarm system,* she realized in panic. But it was impossible. Or had she missed a backup motion sensor? Confused, her nerves jangled by the loud alarm, she didn't know what to do and almost ran. Then, on sheer reflex, she opened the window wide and jumped inside. Batman and Robin were both staring at her through the gloom.

The alarm abruptly went silent. Doors banged open in different walls. The lights blinked and blazed on. Freakishly masked men were rushing at them, pulling guns.

And it's all my fault . . .

She darted behind a jumble of boxes as the first shots exploded and echoed through the factory. She moved swiftly through the maze of skids, determined to make up for her lapse, to summon the warrior spirit, the key to Batgirl. She took a jagged route, hoping to circle behind some of the masked men — "False Facers," Gordon had called them, members of the Black Mask gang, whoever Black Mask was.

She turned a corner. Yes, there were three of them, creeping up a wide aisle away from her, guns in their hands, searching for someone to shoot.

She took three steps and launched herself at full speed. Her flying kick took the rearmost thug in the back, driving him forward into the others. Three guns clattered across the cement floor.

The masked men — smiling Comedy, weeping Tragedy,

and a tribal witch doctor — struggled to rise. Three karate chops changed their minds.

Batgirl kicked the guns farther away, then leaped up to catch the edge of a box. She hauled herself to the top of the loaded skid. Now she was above the maze. So was Batman, about fifty feet away. She watched him drop out of sight down into an aisle. There was a single shot, followed by the thudding sounds of fists and feet. *Good,* she thought, *he wasn't hurt . . .*

From her high vantage point, Batgirl scanned every aisle she could see. There was no sign of Robin, nor could she spot any more of the masked thugs.

She ran to the edge of the skid and leaped across an aisle to the opposite skid. A few boxes crashed behind her, but she didn't care. Desperate now, hoping her mistake wouldn't be costly, she was determined to pay the price. She moved to the edge of the skid and looked down a perpendicular aisle. From here, she could see several of the False Facers moving along an assembly line of metal rollers near the far wall. She headed in their direction, leaping stealthily from one stacked skid to the next, always landing softly, careful not to dislodge any more boxes.

She reached the edge of the last skid. Again it was a trio. They were on the other side of the assembly line, turned away, still unaware of her.

Batgirl took a small, weighted capsule from her belt.

Then she dropped, landing as softly as she could, crouching to absorb and minimize impact.

But all three masked men whirled as one: a scar-stitched Frankenstein monster, a skull face, and a huge-eyed alien. Each held a gun, two black revolvers and one silver automatic. They were going to use them.

Batgirl hurled the weighted capsule to the floor under the assembly line. The capsule popped and then hissed. She was already lunging forward when thick smoke exploded upward and three shots punched holes through it.

"Over there!"

"Look out!"

"I can't see!"

Batgirl vaulted over the assembly line, through the billowing smoke, and slammed into Frankenstein. She rolled up to her feet. The three men were nothing but dark shapes moving in confusion through the haze, completely disoriented. But she was the master of this confusion. It was her ally. She had practiced under these conditions countless times in the cave, and she knew precisely what to do.

"Where is —"

"There! Over there!"

Three more shots rang out, harshly ricocheting off metal surfaces. All three men were doing their best to murder her. She backed off and flattened in the thickest smoke.

Seething with anger, understanding why Batman

loathed guns, she pushed off and moved in low, rising only when she could kick two weapons in rapid succession.

"Hey! My gun —!"

Now only the alien was armed, but the smoke was already thinning and she had to work fast. She grabbed the alien's arm and twisted hard. He yelped in surprise and she banged his wrist down on the metal rollers. The gun flew from his hand and clacked to the floor. She jerked the arm up and then downward again with a twisting motion, using a judo move to pinwheel the alien into Frankenstein.

The swirling haze was almost gone, and with it the elements of surprise and confusion. A grotesque skeleton mask thrust into view, looking like Halloween plastic. She smashed it with a palm thrust and was immediately sorry; the mask was far more solid than it looked. But at least its wearer was dazed. Batgirl leaped into a spin-kick that sent the skeleton mask flying and revealed an even uglier face beneath. She finished the thug with an elbow to the jaw.

There was a shot from the other side of the factory, somewhere in the maze of skids, followed by the sounds of distant fighting. Batman or Robin, maybe both. *Please,* she thought, *don't let them get hurt.*

Then she turned to look for the two remaining thugs. The alien was holding his arm in pain, still down on one knee, but Frankenstein had found a crowbar.

Batgirl dropped into a defensive crouch, ready to ward

off a blow from any direction, but at the same time wondering about the wisdom of blocking metal with bone. Then Frankenstein made his move, swinging the crowbar viciously. Batgirl stepped within the whistling arc, pivoting her left forearm up to chop Frankenstein's wrist. The crowbar glanced off her back, bruise-hard but breaking nothing. It clanked to the floor as she dug a right hook into Frankenstein's ribs. He doubled over and staggered back.

Batgirl was livid now. The man had tried to crush her skull. She moved after him — but was forced to dodge back as Robin cannonballed out of nowhere, his whipping cape clearing the last of the smoke as he deftly landed in her path.

"Filthy habit," he said, "all this smoking — but you rang, Madam?" He executed a courtly bow.

"No, I didn't," Batgirl replied, her jaw set hard. She was still angry, and in no mood for antics of any kind.

"Then it's a good thing I noticed you needed help."

"I *don't* need help," she snapped. All she needed was a clear path to the brute who had tried to brain her.

"Never fear," Robin said, "not when the Boy Wonder is here." And he abruptly kissed her cheek with mock chivalry. She was so stunned she almost smacked him.

But Robin was already spinning away, plowing into Frankenstein.

There was a whirring sound off to Batgirl's right. She

turned to see the alien some thirty feet down the assembly line, almost comically trying to escape. He had jumped atop the metal rollers and his feet were now frantically slipping and skidding as he fought for balance.

On the assembly line next to Batgirl was a box, probably awaiting inspection by the morning shift. She slapped her gloved hands on the box and shoved it down the line as hard as she could. The well-oiled rollers spun freely and the box nearly flew over them. It slammed into the alien's ankles, smacking his feet right out from under him. He looked like a cartoon clown after a close encounter with a banana peel. Heels over head, he bounced off the assembly line and hit the floor hard. He did not get up.

Standing over the felled Frankenstein, Robin was flashing a grin. The need for Batgirl's warrior spirit had passed, but Barbara was still seething. She stalked straight at Robin and stiff-armed his chest, forcing him to lurch back. "Hey!" he said.

"I didn't *need* any help," Barbara said, "and I didn't *ask* for any help!"

"Easy, girl," Robin said.

"I can finish my own fights," Barbara snarled, "and don't call me 'girl'!" She stabbed a finger in his face.

He held up both palms, backing away. "Okay, okay. I was just having a little fun, that's all."

"Being clubbed and shot at is *not fun!* Now just stay out of my —"

A deep voice cut her short: "Enough."

Barbara turned to find Batman right behind her. He was good at that, a living shadow, able to move in total silence, to materialize at will and disappear whenever necessary. "Drop it," he said. "Both of you."

But Barbara's ears were still burning. Unable to control herself, she blurted, "But you don't know what he —"

"Now."

She fell silent, but Batman continued staring at her for several long seconds. Finally he said, "You went directly into the line of fire."

"It was my fault they found us," Barbara tried to explain. "I was trying to make up for —"

"You never go head-on against guns."

"But —"

"Never."

Barbara knew he was right. She also knew she was angry with herself and simply trying to take it out on the others — on the masked thugs, on Robin, even on Batman. But knowing this did not ease her anger, and she had to force herself to stop arguing.

Batman moved past her to the sprawled alien. He knelt and removed the weird mask. There was miniature electronic circuitry in the forehead area of its inner surface.

"Just like all the other masks," he murmured. Then he pried something from the recessed slot and held it up to the light. It was a small square button.

A mystery chip.

Back in the cave, as Batman and Robin hunched over a dozen weird masks spread across a table in the crime-lab area, Barbara was still biting her tongue. The two men seemed utterly oblivious to her presence, unaware of her existence.

Still fuming, she turned away from the light and strode off into one of the Batcave's gloomier areas. She really needed to cool off.

Soon she found herself in a dimly lit hall of trophies. It was an array of bizarre displays, reminders of past encounters with Gotham's most grotesque villains. She had seen the trophies and mementos before, but had never really studied them. A gigantic Joker playing card hanging from the ceiling, a mannequin with one side of its face ripped and ruined, trick umbrellas and robotic penguins, a huge Lincoln penny, a hat studded with question marks, Catwoman's leather whip, a sci-fi freeze-gun, an enormous stuffed dinosaur . . .

Soon the masks would be here too. It all seemed so strange to Barbara. Obsessive. Creepy.

She backed away and brushed against the cold tip of a low-hanging stalactite. It disturbed a flurry of actual bats, suddenly alive and all around her. She flinched away and watched them flutter off into deeper darkness. To her, they always seemed like jagged shreds of blackness torn from a nightmare, and she suddenly realized why: They were the dark and dreaded totems of the Bat*man,* but they were hardly familiar to *her.* And they could never be comforting. She shuddered, feeling lost and alone in the cavern's vast gloom. She was still an outsider, perhaps even an invader.

She turned and headed back for the light.

Each and every mask had a mystery chip implanted in its miniature circuitry. "E.D.O.M.," Batman said. "Perhaps even R.H.I.C."

Robin looked at his mentor as if he'd just sprouted a second head. "Eedeeoem?" the youth echoed. "What are you —"

Barbara cleared her throat and made both of them turn. "You know," she said, "I'm starting to feel left out around here. Not needed."

She waited, but Batman said nothing. Robin made a face at her.

"Like an intruder," she continued, "in the exclusive boys' club of the Batcave."

Obsessed with the problem at hand, Batman clearly had no time for this. "Then perhaps you should focus your energies outside this cave," he said. "And since you plan to major in computers, I can arrange for you to intern at WayneTech for the summer."

Barbara gaped at him, stunned, but his mask gave away nothing — almost frightened her, in fact. She looked at Robin, who shrugged back at her, obviously unwilling to intervene. Was he jealous of her? Resentful that Batman had taken on a second partner?

It didn't matter. They were leaving her no way out, other than backing down and denying her feelings. And that was something she simply couldn't and wouldn't do.

Slowly, returning Batman's stare, she reached up to her head and removed the mask of Batgirl. "Yes," said Barbara Wilson, "perhaps I *should* leave this cave."

Then she turned and stalked off for the rock-carved stairs to Wayne Manor, simply letting the mask fall to the cave floor.

CHAPTER 4
FRESH STARTS

The grandfather clock was a doorway between two worlds, a secret passage from the darkness of the Batcave to the bright lights of Wayne Manor. In the costume vault at the bottom of the rock-carved stairs, Barbara had shed the sleek skin of her Batgirl costume for the last time. Now, in her street clothes at the top of those stairs, she worked a hidden catch and pushed on the back of the tall clock. It swung smoothly inward on silent hinges.

She stepped into the manor's Great Hall, shutting the clock behind her, the measured movement of its pendulum making the only sounds she could hear. She looked around, feeling alone even up here. The butler was now the only anchor left for her.

She began moving through the elegant manor, looking for him, listening for the familiar sound of his soft humming.

He was in the parlor, but he was not humming. Instead,

his manner was solemn as he carefully dusted the large portrait of Bruce's parents, Thomas and Martha Wayne, hanging above the mantel. His chore finished, the butler stepped back and gazed up at the portrait in silence. It was all he had left of the two people he had served so faithfully.

Respecting the moment, Barbara softly cleared her throat only after the elderly man had finally turned away from the portrait. He looked over at her and smiled warmly, his eyes twinkling. He was genuinely delighted to see her, and it was a profound contrast to the treatment she'd been receiving elsewhere.

"Alfred," she said, "I think we have to talk."

"Certainly, Barbara," he said, shooting his cuffs, then tugging down on the points of his vest, making himself the picture of perfect dignity. "Is anything the matter, dear?"

"Yes . . . you could say that, I guess." She paused, and then simply told him, "I just quit."

The butler was appalled.

Alfred Pennyworth had arrived from England when Bruce Wayne was just a boy, and had dutifully served the Wayne family ever since. He had been there when Thomas and Martha Wayne were brutally and tragically gunned down on the street in front of their young son. He had comforted Bruce through his parents' funeral. He had witnessed the youth's bitter vow to wage war on crime, to devote his wealth and his life to that war, to prevent the murder of other victims and therefore the trauma endured by their survivors. It was that very trauma which had shattered young Bruce's life; the boy had resolved to put the pieces back together to form a new and very different man. Alfred had attended the entire process, overseeing the long and arduous studies and training, secretly fearful but outwardly encouraging. He'd seen that he could never change his young master's mind, so great was Bruce's focus and determination; therefore Alfred had sought to strengthen that mind with whatever advice and wisdom he could impart.

Ultimately, the butler had been there for the birth of the Bat, and for the Batman's evolution from rough-and-tumble beginner to world's best in every phase of what he did. He had seen him grow from detective to manhunter to streetfighter, willing to use wits, skill, fear, and even force when necessary. Batman became Gotham's guardian and avenging conscience — and Alfred had somehow become his guide, mentor, and servant all at once. Their mission together was not an easy thing to describe, let alone explain, but now, in the soothing confines of Wayne Manor's parlor, Alfred was attempting to do just that — to explain the mystery that was the Batman.

"You must understand, Barbara," he said patiently, "that the Master has *become* the Bat for all intents and purposes, and that Bruce Wayne has become the mask. I know it seems it should be the other way around, but it's not. So extreme is the Master's dedication to his chosen cause — at times bordering on obsession — that it has almost overwhelmed any desire for a normal life. At this point, Bruce Wayne is little more than a cover for his true pursuits as the Batman."

Barbara watched as the elderly butler, sweetly sincere, waved his hand toward the parlor's walls and ceiling. "Even this stately manor itself, in a very real sense, has become nothing but a mask for the Batcave concealed beneath it. So while you are indeed a ward of Bruce Wayne, you see, it is the Batman who —"

"I appreciate what you're trying to say, Alfred." Barbara leaned forward in her chair to place a hand on the man's arm. "I think I even understand it. But maybe *his* obsession is not *mine*. You've been here so long that you're totally *into* it — as important to him as Robin is, maybe even more so. But this is all new to me, and *mega*-strange." She paused to gesture helplessly. "I mean, it's not like I don't despise crime or anything, but . . . well, my parents were *not* gunned down." She looked away. "And yet, they *are* dead . . ."

"Barbara," Alfred said solemnly, "if you only knew how much I regret —"

"I *do* know, Alfred. You and Mother were once in love, after all."

Alfred's eyes went distant. "She was a wonderful woman . . ."

"And you're a wonderful man. You've supported me ever since Mom and my stepfather died in the car accident. And now you're helping me start a new life here in Gotham, here in this manor. It's just that . . . maybe I should start getting on with that new life."

"But Barbara, you've already made a splendid beginning as Batgirl, and —"

"Sorry, Alfred, but let's agree to disagree. In my opinion, Batgirl is just not working out. In fact, she's practically a disaster."

"But if you could just try to understand the Batman's motivations. He may be a harsh taskmaster, but he's merely trying to —"

Barbara held up a hand to stop him. "Alfred, you're like an uncle to me, and I love you. But I'm really not interested in the inner workings of a full-grown man who swoops and runs through the shadows dressed up like a bat."

Alfred simply gaped at her. She rose from her chair and bent over to gently kiss his head. Then she spoke softly into his ear: "Believe me, I'm extremely grateful to Bruce Wayne for taking me in — and more power to his other half too. Lord knows Gotham needs a dark angel." She straightened. "I'm just not sure *I'm* cut out to be a bat. I love living here in the manor and I want to stay, but as for the rest of it, no thanks. I mean, hanging by my toes from some clammy stalactite when there's a nice cozy bed upstairs? I don't think so. Good night, Alfred, and thanks anyway for trying."

She smiled and turned away, leaving the normally unflappable Alfred with his mouth open but at a complete loss for words.

Barbara trudged up the stairs to the manor's second floor. Despite her firmness with Alfred, she was already second-guessing her decision. Had she done the right thing? How had the situation gotten so complicated in the first place?

Her debut outing as Batgirl had been sheer impulse in the face of an emergency — to help Batman and Robin save Gotham from icy destruction at the hands of three psychotic villains who called themselves Mr. Freeze, Poison Ivy, and Bane. She'd had no time for self-doubt. But the emergency had long since passed. Now that she'd had time to reflect, to experience the long-term reality of being Batgirl, she wasn't sure her original impulse was wise. Oh, she was good enough as Batgirl, and getting better each time she braved the night, but was Batgirl good for her? It was such a dark secret, the beginning of a life lived in danger and shadows . . .

And more exciting than anything I've ever known.

She entered her room and flopped across the bed, sinking deeper into her confused and conflicted funk. *If I'm not Batgirl,* she thought, *then who am I?* Even as Barbara Wilson, she felt adrift in a strange land. Everything had changed. Her parents were gone. She was living with virtual strangers (except for Alfred) in a different country, a different city, and she would be going to a different school in the fall. Even this house seemed alien; the manor was so huge that she could still get lost looking for a bathroom. Her entire life had seemed foreign ever since she'd arrived here from Oxbridge Academy in England. It was a whole new world, a dangerous one, and maybe donning the mantle of a weird creature like Batgirl was actually a logical response.

But it was too late now. The die had been cast when she'd let her mask fall to the floor of the cave. She had quit. She was Barbara Wilson again, plain and simple, a normal human being with normal troubles but no secret identity.

She let her head drop. Maybe all she needed was some quality time with her pillow.

Barbara had just started dozing when there was a soft knock on her door. She roused herself. "Uh . . . come in?"

Dick Grayson entered, looking nervous and not at all

like the flashy, swaggering daredevil who wore the Robin costume. "Hi," he said. "Truce?"

"Sure," she replied sheepishly. "Sorry I shoved you like that back in the factory. Guess I've got a pretty hot head at times."

"Join the club." Dick smiled. Then he turned more serious. "And speaking of similarities between us, I . . . uh . . . I know exactly what you're going through. Trying to fit in as new member of the team and all."

Then he wasn't jealous, she thought, and his sincerity actually made him appealing.

"I went through it myself," Dick continued, "when I first became Robin. And in some ways I'm still going through it. Batman can be a real hard case, Barbara, but he has to be. What you're experiencing right now is understandable, but I think I've been around long enough to offer some advice . . ."

Barbara couldn't believe it. Just like that, Dick was playing the big shot, puffing himself up just so he could talk down to her. And to think she had almost fallen for his charm.

"I can help you avoid the mistakes *I* made," Dick was saying, like he was Santa Claus with a sack full of presents. "I can ease the way, show you the ropes, help you become a true member of the team."

Barbara decided to shock him. "Hold it, Dick," she said.

"What makes you think any of this is important to me? Who said I *wanted* to be on your precious team? Putting that mask on was a whim, not a career move. Go back to your little boys' club down in that clammy cave and forget about Batgirl. You don't need her anyway. I'm Barbara Wilson again — and if you'll just butt out of my business, I could use some rest."

Dick Grayson backed out of the room. His eyes were wide in disbelief.

Bruce Wayne sat at his desk in the manor's library, immersed in a thick text on electronics. He looked up as Alfred entered, bearing juice and sandwiches on a pewter tray. "How is she taking it, Alfred?"

The older man set the tray on the edge of the desk. He still looked grave. "Entirely too passively, sir, for my liking."

Bruce drained half the juice in a single quaff. "She'll come around," he said. "She's got too much spine to take no for an answer."

But Alfred was still troubled. "Unless no is the answer she wants, sir."

Bruce reached for a sandwich. "Which would solve everything." He took a large bite, then shook his head as he chewed. "But I don't believe it. She's already had a taste of the night, and she took to it like a shadow born. Whether she knows it or not, Alfred, there's no way she can turn her back on it forever."

"Then why put her through this game in the first place, sir?"

Bruce turned severe. "It's *not* a game, Alfred. It's deadly serious, and that's the reason. But she's got to realize it — and learn it — for herself. I need partners, not children." He attacked the rest of his sandwich grimly.

"And yet, sir," Alfred said, "you *are* a father figure to them."

"As Bruce Wayne, yes, and I'm here for them. But as Batman, I'm motherless and fatherless and I've got to be childless. Batman is the scourge of the night, Alfred, a dark force of nature which brooks nothing in its path. There are only two choices for Dick and Barbara. They either ride the same whirlwind . . . or they get blown away."

Bruce finished the sandwich and turned back to his book. The conversation was over, and he had already begun something new. It was the way he did everything. Fully, completely, and always with a fresh start.

CHAPTER 5

BIG THINGS

"The first thing you must understand," Roman Sionis said, "is that the most advanced computer in the world is a total idiot."

The WayneTech Company was housed in a large gothic building whose exterior gargoyles of medieval design protected an interior of gleaming futurism. Site of some of the most advanced computer equipment on the planet, WayneTech was an ideal place to learn on the job, and an internship here was every computer student's dream.

Located just beyond the heart of the city, the building was some twenty minutes from Wayne Manor by motorcycle, always Barbara's vehicle of choice.

"And yet the *power* of that computer," Sionis continued, "is incredible, making its creators seem even *lower* than idiots as it performs enough calculations per second to daunt a thousand human brains. That is the paradox which WayneTech's Compu-Link program seeks to address."

"Now, my fine young sub-idiots," Sionis intoned with a smile, "how do we turn the moron which is smarter than us into a genius?"

Arriving early, Barbara had spent some time getting to know the three fellow interns who were also here for their first day on the job. And now, in one of the main labs, the four of them were listening to a welcoming speech by their new boss, the head of WayneTech's Compu-Link program.

"No one wishes to hazard a guess?" Roman Sionis coaxed. "The computer is a brilliant idiot that can run rings around us in many ways. How do we make it even smarter?"

Barbara looked at the other three interns. They seemed clueless, so she decided to speak up: "By using the human brain's one advantage over computers?"

"Which is?" Sionis encouraged.

"The ability to reason? To weigh choices and make decisions?"

"Very good, Ms. Wilson," Sionis said. "We must teach the computer to think as well as calculate. Right now, computers do one thing very well and that is what makes them brilliant. The fact that they can't do much else is what makes them dumb. The limited human brain, on the other hand, is far more versatile. Even though it cannot hope to compete on the computer's specialized level, it can do many things very well, and that is what makes it superior.

The human mind, after all, created the computer — but I can't imagine a computer creating Albert Einstein."

Barbara was fascinated. The other interns looked at her as she spoke again. "Then the Compu-Link program's goal is to design a computer that functions like the human brain?"

Roman Sionis was visibly pleased. "Precisely, Ms. Wilson," he said. "And the key is literally within our own heads. We talk of making computers more 'user-friendly,' but that is possible only if the users are actual friends. And I don't know about you, but I find it extremely difficult to become friends with a cold, dumb machine."

"Sometimes," one of the interns cracked, "I want to punch my laptop."

"Or pitch the thing right out a window," another agreed.

"Exactly," Sionis responded. "So we must establish common ground in the interface between human and machine. The gulf between us must be bridged. And since no human wants to become more like a machine, we must force the machine to become more like a human."

"Mr. Sionis," Barbara said, "can you tell us how WayneTech is approaching this problem?"

"Pretty much by groping in the dark, Ms. Wilson. Since the workings of the human mind remain largely a mystery, we really don't know *how* to approach it. But we are trying two things. First is brute force." Sionis swept a hand around the lab, indicating the awesome array of mainframe computers, all state of the art. "And second is a primitive mimicry of the one human brain process we do understand . . ."

"Parallel linkage of all these mainframes?" Barbara asked.

Sionis looked at her. "Now I *am* impressed, Ms. Wilson. Your deduction is quite correct. Normal computer processing functions in serial fashion — in a line, as it were, to perform calculations from one step to the next. We think this is clumsy and laborious. So we want to devote all the enormous power of each mainframe to a separate, specialized task. Then we hope to force them all to work together at the same time — in tandem — to create a synergy, a whole that is greater than the sum of its individual parts."

"Almost like a hive mind," one of the other interns said, "which amounts to a single human intelligence?"

"Indeed," Sionis replied, "but without the human mind's capacity for independence. We want decision-making, but not to the point of disobedience. Whatever we do, we must ensure that these computers remain machines, enslaved to a master controller — to the human operator's commands. After all, we don't want mentally superior entities suddenly deciding we're too dumb to run the world."

"Even if it's true?" asked one of the interns.

"Especially since it's true," Barbara said, and they all laughed, including Roman Sionis.

"You'll learn more details as we go along," he said. "Now let's tame and train some brains, shall we?"

"Are you talking about the computers," Barbara asked, "or *our* brains?"

"Both." Sionis smiled. "Although I'm not sure which will prove more difficult."

By the end of Barbara's first day, the other interns were calling her Teacher's Pet. It suited her just fine.

And by the end of her first week, Barbara was on a first-name basis with her boss. Roman seemed to think the world of her, and spoke glowingly of her aptitude for computer work. "Barbara," he said, "you could have a real future with WayneTech, preferably right here with me. You already understand this program on an intuitive level, better than some of the techs who've been here for years."

Barbara beamed with pride. Batgirl seemed long ago and far away.

Meanwhile, even as Barbara was enjoying her success at WayneTech, Gotham suffered an all-out crime wave launched by the Black Mask gang. Night after night, Batman and Robin arrived at crime scenes just moments too late. And even when several of the crimes were foiled, resulting in the capture of more False Facers, the onslaught continued unabated. There were simply too many criminals, and no way for the two heroes to be everywhere at once.

"The Black Mask gang has grown too large," Batman said sternly. "At this point, criminals are flooding into Gotham from other cities just to join up. It's like fighting the many tentacles of the mythical Hydra."

"This Hydra," Robin said. "Anybody ever stop it?"

"Only by cutting off its head."

"And in our case, the head is —"

"Black Mask himself."

Robin sighed. "I knew you'd say that."

But the Dark Knight was even more disturbed by the targets of certain crimes: special generators, advanced technology specs and blueprints, transmitting and receiving devices. They were unusual items to steal, and suggested a motive beyond mere greed or profit. "Black Mask is collecting things," he decided, "with a greater goal in mind. Something big."

"Bigger," Robin wanted to know, "than this full-scale mega–crime wave?"

"Yes," Batman replied with certainty. "A lot bigger."

Three nights later, the inhabitants of Wayne Manor were in the dining room finishing their soup. It was the second week of Barbara's internship at WayneTech, and her relations with Bruce and Dick were cordial but chilly. Bruce had not even mentioned Batgirl since that last night in the cave, and Dick hadn't said another word on the subject either, not since their disastrous talk in Barbara's room.

Alfred entered from the kitchen, carrying a large serving platter and wearing a look of understated woe. "The main course, Master Bruce," he said, "but I'm afraid it's just been spoiled by a certain signal in the sky."

Bruce was out of his chair like a shot, not even looking out the dining room windows as he headed straight for the main hall and the grandfather clock. It was time for the Batman.

Dick also rose quickly, but paused to snatch a potato from Alfred's platter and look across the table at Barbara. "Still playing hard to get?" he asked. "Or do you want to join us again?"

"No, thanks," Barbara said. "I'm going back to WayneTech tonight. Roman asked me to put in some overtime on the Compu-Link program." Then she dabbed napkin to mouth, smiling sweetly but with her eyes hard and glittering. "And golly gee," she added, "looks like I'll get a second helping tonight."

Dick's face was sour as he waved a hand in dismissal, stuffed the potato into his mouth, and hustled after Bruce.

"Alfred," Barbara said, "let's eat."

The butler wearily shook his head.

"No emergency," Commissioner Gordon said, "and nothing new to report." He was pacing in front of the rooftop beacon, shoulders hunched in his light trench coat.

"I don't get it," Robin said. "Then why'd you slap the Bat-Signal on the sky?"

"I'm not really sure," Gordon answered. "Just antsy, I guess. As you say, Batman, Black Mask is building up to something big, and we still don't have a clue. The whole thing has been eating at me."

"Wish *we* were eating at something," Robin muttered.

Batman shot him a look. "Go on, Commissioner."

"Well . . . we've had the first batch of False Facers in custody for two weeks now, and nothing's changed. They're still acting like zombies. Won't give up so much as their names. They claim they can't even *remember* their names."

"Are they still being kept here at headquarters — in holding cells?"

"Until their trial," Gordon said, "yes."

"And your evidence room is just down the hall?"

"Yes."

"And their masks are being stored in that evidence room?"

Gordon stopped pacing, wondering what Batman was getting at. "Except for the masks you took, yes."

"Then I don't think they're acting," Batman said. "I suspect they're telling the truth. They probably *can't* remember their own names."

Gordon thrust his chin out. "What are you getting at?"

"E.D.O.M., Commissioner. And R.H.I.C."

Robin snapped his head. He'd forgotten all about those two strange terms. Batman had been on the verge of explaining them when Barbara interrupted with her melodramatic resignation as Batgirl, killing all further discussion in the cave.

"You're talking about *what?*" Gordon said.

"Two very evil mind-control programs," Batman explained, "practiced by various spy agencies." His eyes grew distant and he slowly made fists before continuing. "E.D.O.M. stands for electronic dissolution of memory, a process in which electromagnetic waves are used to literally erase a subject's personality. And R.H.I.C. stands for radio-hypnotic intracerebral control, in which other waves interfere with a subject's brainwave patterns — and actually take control of brain functions."

Gordon was incredulous. "You mean the False Facers are nothing but remote-controlled robots? And the control waves are coming from those 'mystery chips' in the masks?"

Batman nodded.

"But if you're right," Gordon went on, "why haven't my officers been affected by the masks? Why haven't *we* been affected?"

"I'm not sure," Batman admitted, "but I suspect the E.D.O.M. waves are emitted only for a short period after the masks are first activated. That's probably what does all the damage. After that, the masks' chips may shift to a different maintenance frequency — harmless to anyone who hasn't undergone the initial phase. Try moving the masks from the evidence room, out of range of the prisoners. They may come to their senses and start talking, but I wouldn't count on it. My guess is, their memories have been destroyed forever. Along with their ability to think."

Gordon gaped at him. "They're brain-dead?"

"Not in a medical sense," Batman replied, "but close enough."

Robin let out a long, low whistle. If Batman was right, then Black Mask really *was* dealing in big things.

CHAPTER 6
DAWNING DREAD

Barbara liked Roman Sionis, but she had to admit her boss could be slightly weird at times. He looked to be in his late twenties, as far as she could tell, yet he often acted a lot older. Maybe it was the strange air of intensity that could come over him without warning. And while he was good-looking on the surface — tall, athletically built, dark hair and eyes, somewhat rough but handsome features — there was something within him that sometimes caused a visible change, and not always for the better. Then there was that odd wandering of his eyes, as if he were searching for sights only he could see, and the way he would hunch over and get lost in vague mutterings. It had actually spooked Barbara on several occasions.

But even though the total effect could be unsettling, she was willing to chalk it up to nothing more than a series of quirks and eccentricities. Roman Sionis was, after all, the cyberspace equivalent of a mad scientist, wasn't he? And he was certainly a genius. Why else would Bruce Wayne pay him so much to head up the Compu-Link program? So a little weirdness came with the package — no big deal.

Tonight, however, Barbara was really beginning to wonder about Roman. He was creeping her out way more than usual, whistling off-key, abruptly smacking the side of a mainframe and laughing out loud, humming and singing strange tunes that she had never heard, that probably no one had ever heard.

Maybe it was only because they were working after hours, alone in the huge WayneTech lab. Maybe Roman was just feeling loose. He was definitely feeling expansive. "You know, Barbara," he suddenly said.

She looked up from her work, startled by the loudness of his voice.

"In one way, I really envy computers."

"Ah . . . what way is that, Roman?"

He clucked his tongue, not even looking at her. In fact, he had yet to look in her direction at all, instead staring fixedly at the array of mainframes. "Computers have *no fears,* of course!" He gestured toward them. "No worries or obscssions, Barbara, no distracting thoughts to get in the way of the task at hand. They have *no emotions at all.*"

It should have been a joke, but he seemed so serious that Barbara didn't quite know how to respond. She decided to treat it lightly, if not with a laugh. "But Roman . . . haven't you just listed practically everything that makes us human?"

"Precisely, Barbara! And wouldn't it be wonderful to be *free of it all?* Nothing but clean, cool intellect? No messy feelings? Wouldn't that be wonderful, Barbara?"

"Not for me, Roman," she said. "Not at all."

He finally whirled and stared right through her, his eyes huge. "But just think, Barbara! Think if we could reach the brain's slate and wipe it clean — reprogram our minds from the neurons up!" He was working his hands wildly, trying to grab the concept out of thin air and shape it into something real.

Barbara was more than nervous now and tried to choose her words carefully. "But you've said it yourself, Roman. The brain is not a machine."

"But it could be," he snapped. "A miraculous machine of unlimited potential! And if enough of these miraculous machines were linked in parallel — every brain in Gotham, for example, millions of brilliant drones all serving a single master controller — think of what might be accomplished!" He lunged right at Barbara and pounded his fist down on her desk. "And with the right kind of radionics and delivery system, it could actually be done, Barbara! A signal of the proper frequency transmitted into every —"

Roman stopped short, as if just realizing the effect his words were having. "Sorry," he said, his voice now meek and quiet. "I sometimes get carried away in my flights of fancy. Nothing but pipe dreams, of course." And then he tried to laugh the whole thing off.

Barbara tried to laugh along, but knew it sounded hollow. Feigning a headache, she excused herself early and quickly left the lab and the building.

Outside, kicking her motorcycle to life, she was still left with an uncomfortable feeling. She had just seen a mask slip, and the face underneath had frightened her to the bone.

She gunned the throttle, shifted gears, and shot out into the night.

Barbara arrived back at Wayne Manor to find Alfred waiting up for her. "Since Masters Bruce and Dick are, ah, still out," the butler said, "I thought we might have a talk, Barbara. I could even make some cocoa . . ."

Barbara wanted to beg off, to be alone while she thought through what had happened at the lab, but Alfred was clearly troubled and she just couldn't refuse the dear sweet man. "Sure," she said, following him to the kitchen. "What do you want to talk about?"

"Actually," he said, "I'm rather concerned about Masters Bruce and Dick pushing themselves too hard. Why, just tonight — you saw — they didn't even eat." He started warming milk for the cocoa. "It's this Black Mask

business, of course, and it's getting entirely out of hand."
He seemed more than concerned, and almost angry.

Barbara took two mugs from a cabinet. "How so?" she
asked absently, still dwelling on Roman's strange behavior.

"Why, the crime wave, dear. Haven't you been following the news? Black Mask's gang has grown to the size of
a small army. And did you know that each and every one of
them is apparently a puppet?"

Barbara spooned cocoa into the mugs. "Did you say
puppet, Alfred?"

"Indeed I did. Evidently, this so-called False Face Society of Gotham lacks all semblance of free will." Alfred
poured steaming milk into the mugs. "Master Bruce feels
they are much like 'drones in a hive mind,' all controlled
by Black Mask — obviously through those mysterious
chips in their masks."

Barbara was abruptly chilled, suddenly alert.

"If only the Master knew who Black Mask *is* . . ."

"Tell me more," Barbara said. She knew Alfred was trying to coax her back into the cave. It wouldn't work, but
now — for her own reasons — she did want to hear what
he had to say. "Tell me everything."

And he did, almost lecturing about ELF waves and
E.D.O.M. and R.H.I.C., about the strange nature and odd
targets of certain crimes, and the fact that not a single False
Facer could remember so much as his own name.

Some of it Barbara was already aware of, but much of it was new to her. It was also disturbing, and all too familiar. Dark suspicions shot through her mind as she listened, and by the time Alfred started winding down, she was almost certain.

"So you see, dear, it's become quite a distressing problem. Masters Bruce and Dick could certainly use some assistance on this one, and I thought perhaps you might reconsider your decision to —"

"Excuse me, Alfred," Barbara said, "but . . . ah . . . Roman said some things tonight that I need to go over in my room."

The butler seemed crestfallen, but recovered quickly and made a visible effort to brighten. "Then all is going well," he said, "with your work at WayneTech?"

"Uh, yeah," Barbara replied. "It's really . . . well, it's a terrific job." And she left the kitchen, heading for the stairs to her room. "Thanks for the cocoa, Alfred. It was great."

The butler peeked into her mug. She hadn't tasted a drop.

Working overtime at WayneTech — alone after hours with Roman Sionis — was now at the very bottom of Barbara's list of favorite things to do. But she had to know whether her suspicions were right.

Black Mask was using mystery computer chips to accomplish the opposite of Compu-Link's goal as defined by her boss. Instead of making machines function more like the human mind, as Roman Sionis was supposedly trying to do, Black Mask was turning humans into robotic machines. One aspect of both processes was eerily the same, however: the creation of "hive minds" that obeyed a single "master controller." In the case of Black Mask, that controller was evil. Was the same true of Roman Sionis? Was he somehow involved?

She had to know.

And so, when Roman asked her to work late twice in the following week, Barbara accepted both times. But her mind was hardly on the work. Instead, she secretly studied Roman himself, finding new and sinister meaning in each of his various "quirks" and "eccentricities." She also studied the clock, anxiously awaiting the fifteen-minute breaks he took every two hours.

And during each break, as soon as Roman left the lab, Barbara snooped. Her pace was frantic, her heart pounding, as she went about her self-appointed mission. First she left the lab and slipped into the personnel office to read the file on Sionis.

During the next break, she examined Compu-Link's requisition records on a hunch, comparing them with lab inventories. She even skimmed the papers in and on Roman's desk, reading as much as she could, wishing she knew the passwords to his private computer files, imagining his early return at any and every moment. She always had an excuse prepared, ready and waiting to be delivered with perfect innocence if need be. *Oh, hello, Roman. I didn't expect you back so quickly. Listen, I need those specs on the new mainframe hard-drives. Do you know where they might be?*

But she was never caught, and she did not like what she had found. Nevertheless, she tried to be completely objective about each shred of evidence, telling herself it could still be nothing but gigantic coincidence. Unlikely, yes, but innocent just the same.

The capper came during Roman's last break on the second night. Rummaging through his bottom desk drawer, Barbara found a set of Compu-Link blueprints. They were different from the ones she worked with almost every day. They had, in fact, been deliberately altered. But why would Roman modify the circuitry like this, she wondered, unless he planned to *add* something? Maybe something like a mystery chip?

Barbara left WayneTech that night with her mind made up and not a single doubt blocking the way. She was certain she now had what she needed: a single answer to all the questions shaped in dawning dread.

CHAPTER 7
PURSUED CLUES

Barbara returned to the manor and found Bruce Wayne studying in the library. It was late and he looked freshly showered, but she couldn't tell whether he'd just come home or was yet to go out. Where the Batman was concerned, one never knew. Dawn was the only curfew he obeyed.

Bruce acknowledged her presence without looking up. "Barbara." Just her name, halfway between question and statement, nothing else.

She started slowly. "The only way to stop Black Mask is by learning his identity."

"Not the only way," Bruce said, "but the best and quickest way."

Unable to contain herself, Barbara blurted the rest of it right out: "I think I know his real identity. I think Black Mask is my boss and your employee — Roman Sionis."

Now Bruce did look up at her. "That's an extremely serious charge, Barbara."

"I can back it up, Bruce — with evidence."

"Then do so."

It all came out in a rush. Barbara found she couldn't speak fast enough as she told him about the requisitions for expensive electronic equipment — equipment she could find nowhere in the lab. "Not only that," she said, "but it's all advanced transmitting and receiving gear — stuff that doesn't even apply to the Compu-Link program."

Then she told about the three universities she had phoned, the ones Roman Sionis had listed on his job application but that had never heard of him.

And there was also the matter of the blueprints, altered to accommodate something that could easily be a mystery chip.

"WayneTech has never used chips like that," Bruce interrupted.

"And if Roman is planning to use them now," Barbara countered, "you don't think he'd tell anyone, do you?"

"Have you actually *seen* any of those chips in the lab?"

"Well, no, but . . ."

"But what, Barbara?"

"I don't know the details, but I do know that Roman is up to something down at WayneTech. I can feel it in my —"

"Not good enough," Bruce said flatly.

"Look, Bruce, I couldn't believe it either, not at first. I thought it was just one long train of creepy coincidences. But this train has too many cars. It's a mile long. There's definitely something weird and shady about Roman Sionis."

Bruce almost smiled. "You could say the same thing about me, Barbara."

She fumbled at the air, getting frustrated now. "You know what I mean."

Bruce rose and slowly paced along the long bookshelves. Barbara had the impression he was looking for a decision. "Roman may be unusual," he finally said, "and falsifying one's academic record is serious." He stopped and looked at Barbara. "But it does not make him Black Mask."

Barbara was so frustrated she had to bite her tongue. How could she get through to this man? His logic may have been perfectly rational, but it was also perfectly maddening. There had to be some way to convince him, and she had to find it. She looked around and shook her head, trying to rattle the answer loose. Nothing. Bruce was watching her, waiting.

Then it was right in front of her, and she jumped on it. "His own words," she said, feeling like a dolt. Truth wasn't always a collection of cold facts; sometimes it was found in subjective impressions, intuitions, maybe even feelings that bordered on ESP. "All the creepy things he said about computers, Bruce."

"What things, Barbara?"

And she suddenly realized how Bruce would react to any hint of "ESP." As Batman, he relied on his own sixth sense every night. It had saved his life any number of times. But he would never accept it as absolute proof of anything.

"What things?" Bruce repeated.

Too late now, she thought. "Well . . . the first night I worked overtime with him, for instance, he . . . he actually scared me, Bruce. I mean, he really lost it, went right over the edge. Almost raving, you know? He showed this crazy side of himself I'd never seen before. You had to be there, probably, to really understand what I'm —"

"Exactly what did he say, Barbara?"

He was cutting right to the chase, as usual, and for once she didn't blame him. *I sound totally lame,* she thought, *rambling all over the place.* And with a sinking feeling that almost took her breath away, she suddenly knew why: *I have no real proof. In a court of law, I would have exactly zilch. Case dismissed.*

"Barbara?"

There was only one way out, so she took it, plowing straight ahead: "Well, he . . . he made his ultimate goal sound like . . . like *mind control* . . . at least if the program were somehow applied to human brains rather than computers. Which is exactly what Black Mask is doing, isn't it? I mean, Roman was talking about things that sounded a lot like E.D.O.M. and R.H.I.C. and —"

"Dick told you about that?"

Barbara shook her head. "Alfred," she said. "I think he was hoping to keep me involved, maybe even trying to change my mind about —"

"Leave your cycle in the garage tomorrow," Bruce said. "I'll drive you to WayneTech."

Barbara turned away to hide her fierce smile. Somehow, against all odds, she'd done it; she had actually convinced him. She turned back, under control again. "Then you're going to confront Roman and —"

Bruce lifted a hand to stop her. "I'm doing this reluctantly," he said. "Whether or not he has earned genuine degrees in science and engineering, Roman Sionis has always performed well for WayneTech." He paused. "And I'm still less than convinced by the weight of your evidence. But you have uncovered certain things that are too important to ignore. If you're right, lives could be at stake."

"And saved," Barbara said.

"But if you're wrong," Bruce went on, "*Roman's* life could be ruined." He looked directly into her eyes, and the effect was almost electric. "I hope, Barbara, that you are *not wrong.*" Then he stepped right past her and strode from the library, turning in the direction of the grandfather clock.

So his night was just beginning, not ending. But he'd be back before dawn, Barbara knew, with plenty of time to shower again before driving her to WayneTech. Maybe this was the key to his intensity: lack of sleep.

Whatever its source, that intensity could be downright scary. But Barbara wasn't worried about being wrong. She was more certain than ever, in fact, that she was right — and the certainty was exciting. She left the library pumped with pride. She had nailed it, cracking a mystery that had stumped the Darknight Detective himself. And she had done it all as Barbara Wilson, not Batgirl.

Not as a member of some team, but all on her own. As herself.

"Why, yes," Roman Sionis said, "I did requisition that equipment, Mr. Wayne."

From her workstation across the lab, Barbara watched as Bruce played it in neutral fashion, neither smiling nor accusing. "And where is the equipment now, Roman?"

"Well, I . . . I took it home, Mr. Wayne, but only so I could work on a side project during the weekends."

Some side project, Barbara thought. *Turning crooks into zombie slaves . . .*

Roman was digging through one of his desk drawers. "And I think it's starting to pay off well," he said. "Here, have a look, Mr. Wayne." And he extended a thick sheaf of what looked like drawings and notes.

Barbara was immediately suspicious. She desperately wanted a closer look at those notes, but the whole point of remaining at her station was to prevent Roman from realizing she was the cause of Bruce's supposedly impromptu inspection. Still, she glimpsed enough of the papers to know they were something new. She'd gone through Roman's desk twice and had never seen anything like them. Did he already know who was behind this surprise visit by Bruce Wayne? Was Roman aware of her snooping activities all along? And had he prepared his own "innocent excuse" in the form of these notes?

"I just brought them in this morning." Roman was saying. "I got excited by how my idea is coming along, you see, and I thought I might work on it during lunch."

Or was there any possibility — even just one in a zillion — that she was completely and utterly wrong about everything?

Bruce shuffled through the papers. "Some new transceiver system?" he asked.

No, not even one in a zillion. She *couldn't* be wrong.

"Yes," Roman said. "If I can find a way to transmit a

dense enough data stream, we could eliminate the need for modems and phone lines. I know it seems like a step backward in this age of fiber optics, Mr. Wayne, but just think of it — unlimited access to the Internet, and all for free. Or at least free after every user buys a brand-new WayneTech-patented transceiver, of course. If I pull this off, Mr. Wayne, the increased revenue for this company —"

"Would be enormous," Bruce said. "And you'll receive a generous bonus, Roman, I assure you."

Barbara kept her head down and bit her lower lip. Bogus or not, the notes were obviously convincing.

Bruce handed the sheaf of papers back. "Excellent work," he said. "But I'd like to discuss some irregularities in your personnel file, Roman, specifically in your listing of universities and degrees."

Roman looked stunned. "You found out," he said, hanging his head in shame. "I . . . I'm sorry, Mr. Wayne. I never wanted to deceive you *or* the company, but you're right and I admit it . . . I did lie on my job application. I didn't earn any of those degrees . . . never attended those schools. I couldn't afford any of them, not back then." He buried his face in his hands. His shoulders began to tremble. "Everything I learned was from the public library," he said, his voice ready to crack. "But I think I've shown that my knowledge is enough to —"

"More than enough," Bruce said. He put a hand on the man's shoulder to steady him. "Carry on, Roman — and keep up the good work."

Barbara caught Bruce out in the hall. "He's just acting," she hissed. "You can see that, can't you?"

Bruce looked at her, his eyes hard. "What I see," he said very softly, "is that you're not doing so well *outside* the cave either."

Then he was gone, leaving her stung and disbelieving. She wanted to go after him. She wanted to tug on his arm and plead and protest. She wanted to pound a wall and shout the truth. But she knew she couldn't press it, not now, not without absolute proof.

She turned back into the lab, where Roman wore a mask of utter innocence. It would be a long day, and already she couldn't wait for it to end.

Barbara emerged from WayneTech to find Alfred in his livery uniform, standing next to one of Bruce Wayne's vintage limousines. This one was either a Bentley or an antique Rolls-Royce, she wasn't quite sure. Not that it mattered.

Alfred opened the rear passenger door. His slight bow invited her to enter the backseat luxury of buttery leather and polished wood.

Instead, she pushed the door shut. "No, thanks, Alfred," she said. "I'll ride up front, if it's all the same to you. I realize you take pride in your role as chauffeur, but what I really need right now is a friend."

Alfred gave her forehead a quick peck. "At your service," he said.

And so, side by side in the front seat, the rest of the car trailing behind them like some abandoned mansion, they eased out into the afternoon rush hour. "Master Bruce told me what happened this morning," Alfred said. "I imagine that's the source of your upset?"

"Not really," Barbara replied. "I'm clear on that."

"Then you still think your suspicions are correct?"

"I *know* they are."

"And you're stubbornly determined to prove it."

"Yep. So what we need here, my dear Alfred, is just your basic pep talk — with maybe a little advice on where to go from here."

Alfred tooted the horn, alerting a would-be lane-changer to just how long the limo was. "Master Bruce demands a lot from others," he said, "especially from his wards and partners — almost as much as he demands of himself."

"So I've gathered," Barbara said, "and he sure is grim about it. I'm not sure the man has any sense of humor."

Alfred turned grave. "One night in the Master's first year as the Bat," he said, "I found him curled up in the shadows of the cave. He said something which has haunted me from that night to this very day. His face was ashen and bleeding. His cape was torn. There were human bite marks all over both his hands, right through the gloves. His costume was splotched with green and white and purple paint. He never explained any of it."

"What did he say, Alfred?"

"He said . . . 'It's not funny.'"

"That's it?"

"No. He also said, 'After tonight, nothing will ever be funny again.'"

"The Joker?"

"That was my guess too, Barbara, but only later, after I became aware of the Joker. On the other hand, I'm not sure the Joker even existed at the time . . . and as I say, the Master never explained. Indeed, he has never so much as mentioned that night. Sometimes I wonder if it ever really happened . . . or if I simply dreamed the whole thing."

"Dark dream," Barbara said.

"Yes," Alfred said.

"If it did happen, it might explain a lot about his grimness."

"Indeed."

They were both silent for a while.

Finally Barbara said, "What if I remained his ward, Alfred, but not his partner?"

Alfred failed to conceal his twitch of disappointment. "His demands would be fewer," he said, "although no less strict."

"And if I were still his partner?"

"Then you would be part of an enterprise which can ill afford mistakes and which must always strive for perfection." Alfred turned the wheel, expertly guiding the limousine onto the bridge spanning the Gotham River. "What the Master cannot do is waste time as a babysitter or a fretful parent. Anyone wishing to work with him, then, must demonstrate independence — but without being foolhardy and without ever questioning his authority."

"Kind of a fine line, isn't it, if you're in the hero business?"

"No one said it would be easy, Barbara. Indeed, it is rare and special work, and to do it well you must be the same."

"But how would the perfect partner, for example, know where to draw that fine line?"

Alfred considered. "A difficult question," he said, "since every situation is different. And this is precisely the area in which Master Dick had — and still has — the most trouble. Toeing that fine line between initiative and recklessness. Acting alone versus seeking help. There is a time for each approach, you see."

"I get the concept loud and clear, Alfred, but how do you know which time is which?"

"You learn, Barbara. You mature. You develop judgment and instincts."

"Do you think I went to Bruce for help too early this time?"

"Perhaps," Alfred said with an easy and elegant shrug, coming down more on the side of yes than no.

"And yet I went wrong the other way as Batgirl — going against armed goons on my own in the factory."

This time Alfred left no doubt. *"Indeed,"* he said sternly.

"Which leaves us where, Alfred? Those are two guidelines, but what's the wrap-up?"

"Should you decide you want it, Barbara, you shall have to find your own place in the cave. But once you do, you shall never be alone again."

She was still not quite convinced. "If you say so, Alfred."

"Stop thinking of yourself as a mere sidekick, Barbara, but also stop thinking of yourself as an invincible one-woman army. Become a partner. Never act like a child, but neither succumb to overconfident pride. Act decisively, but always know when to call in the cavalry."

Again they rode in silence, Barbara deep in thought, Alfred stealing glances at her. Finally, as they pulled into the long driveway that swept up to Wayne Manor, she reached her decision.

"And yet," she mused to herself, "there's cavalry . . . and there's *cavalry*."

"Eh? What's that, dear?"

"Some words of wisdom for *you*, Sir Alfred," she said excitedly, "inspired by your *magic* word!"

"What magic word?" Alfred was utterly bewildered.

"Cavalry." She grinned. "And never bother the General when a scout will do." Then she leaned over to squeeze Alfred in a monster hug, and jumped from the limo while it was still rolling to a stop. When she sprinted for the front door, wings seemed to blossom from her heels.

Alfred emerged from the limousine more slowly, long after Barbara was already inside. He smartly flicked the bill of his chauffeur's cap and permitted himself a broad smile. "Once again," he said out loud, "the Master had it correct from the start. That girl *does* have too much spine to quit."

Then he twisted his cap all the way around backward and fired a jaunty kick at the limousine's front tire.

Dick Grayson was studying in his room. The door was open, so Barbara stepped inside. He seemed surprised to see her. "Hey," she said, starting out slowly but barely able to contain herself.

"Hey back," Dick replied cautiously.

She nodded at his textbooks. "My calendar must be off," she observed. "It says summer."

"Mine too," he said with a glum smile. "But there's no rest for the wicked."

"Aw, you ain't so bad," she said with a cocky sparring shuffle. Then she tried to make her next words casual and conversational. "So . . . no Bruce around?"

"I don't think so," Dick said. "Mentioned how he was gonna follow some hot new lead tonight."

"Without you?"

Dick indicated the textbooks spread across his desk. "Since my grades slipped last quarter, 'Dad' figured I should hit the books rather than the streets once in a while. Plus I think he's a little ticked off."

"At you too, huh?"

Now Dick's smile turned rueful. "Hey, you're not the only one who can screw up, you know."

Barbara moved deeper into the room. "The Boy Wonder? What did you do, Dick?"

"Nothing major. Just the usual overload of wisecracks and stunts in our last few outings."

"Same old dashing daredevil," Barbara said. "You'll never learn."

He looked up at her with his best cool look. "When you've got the goods," he said, "it's hard not to flaunt 'em."

As if buying none of *that* nonsense, Barbara stiffly perched on the edge of the desk, crossed her arms, and looked down her nose. "In other words, young man," she said in a scolding schoolmarm voice, "you've been slipping off that high wire between initiative and recklessness again."

Dick grinned. "And *you've* been heart-to-hearting with wise old Alfred!"

They both dropped their acts and Barbara suddenly felt closer to Dick. It was only natural; there was no one else like them on earth, no one else who could possibly understand, no one else who had actually brushed capes with the Batman himself.

"Bruce *is* rough on partners," Barbara said, "isn't he?"

"You got that right," Dick agreed, "but it's nothing compared to how he is on criminals."

Barbara's eyes grew distant. "Tell me, Dick," she said, "did *you* ever have doubts . . . in the beginning, I mean?"

"Are you kidding?" He waved a hand at the ceiling. "Only a zillion. And you wanna know a secret?"

"Yeah."

"Just between us?"

"Yeah."

"Goes no further?"

"Sure."

"I still have doubts," Dick said, "every time I slap on the mask."

Barbara nodded. "So it's not just me."

"No way."

"It really *is* a tough job, Dick."

"Yeah, who knows — maybe the toughest."

"I just wish he could see that we're trying . . ."

Bruce's low voice carried the power to shake down pillars. "Trying is good," he said. "Trying is admirable."

Barbara and Dick jumped and whirled. They were riveted by his dark silhouette framed in the doorway.

"But in matters of life and death," Bruce continued, "trying is never enough. Succeeding is the only acceptable goal. You can't expect me to risk your lives if you're not ready."

They strained to see his face, but he was just a dark shape in the gloom.

"I'm not your father, but I *am* responsible for you, and it's a responsibility that is both grave and precious. I'm still convinced Black Mask is building up to something big. I'm about to follow up another lead right now. Whatever he plans to do, lives will surely be threatened. I don't want yours added to the tally."

Barbara had finally swallowed her heart back down where it belonged. "But you can't protect us forever," she said. "What if you need our help to stop Black Mask?"

"You're right," Bruce said, "I *might* need help. But what I *don't* need is the distraction of worrying about you." He paused, took a slow, deep breath. "Dick, you're almost there. At times you *are* there — the perfect partner. Barbara, you're newer. You're still on the edge, and you could go either way. I repeat: This is big, and I can't risk you, either of you." He seemed to look at each of them in turn. "You're too special, both of you."

Then he withdrew his presence and was gone.

Dick let out a long, low whistle. "For *his* heart," he said, "that's as heartfelt as it gets."

Barbara crossed to the doorway and looked up and down the hall. Bruce was gone. She turned back in to the room. "Do you think that could have been his way of *asking* for our help?"

Dick thought for a moment and shrugged. "Maybe. He's always saying he's there for us and all we've gotta do is ask, but I'm not sure *he* could ever come right out and ask for anything."

"Listen," Barbara said urgently, "I think I know who Black Mask is, but I need proof. It's getting dark now. Want to help me take some initiative?"

Dick sized her up. "Any recklessness involved?"

"We could probably find a way to work *some* into the deal . . ."

"But not *too* much," Dick said.

"No, not too much," Barbara agreed. "Never again."

Dick flipped his textbooks shut and stood up from the desk. "Race you," he said, "to the cave."

Barbara emerged from the costume vault feeling more than disguised. She actually felt transformed, finally comfortable in the Batgirl outfit, as if understanding it for the first time.

Wearing it in the past had been mere masquerade, but this time the change was real. This time she *wanted* to be Batgirl. This time she meant it. She had something personal to prove.

"Lookin' sharp," Robin said, buckling his belt, "except for one key item."

"I know," Barbara said, reaching up to touch her face. "The mask."

Robin shook his forefinger at her. "Don't leave home without it."

It was on the cave floor exactly where she had let it fall more than two weeks ago. "But why is it still . . . ?"

"Batman's orders." Robin shrugged. "He said no one had the right to pick it up except you — and only if you wanted it badly enough."

"That stinker," Barbara murmured. "He knew I'd be back all along. He never even accepted my resignation."

She plucked the mask from the floor, dusted it off, and put it back in place, where it belonged.

Robin looked at Batgirl and nodded righteously, as if perfect balance had finally been restored to the universe.

Capes flowing, they moved off for their vehicles, ready to dare the darkness and pursue clues.

CHAPTER 8
ZOMBIE CITY

Batman stood in shadows at the base of the gothic WayneTech building. He raised his left arm and there was a hushed *chuff* as his wrist-grapnel shot upward, trailing its line. A soft *clank,* and it was hooked over the deformed snout of a hideous gargoyle. Batman tested his weight on the line and found the grip secure. Swiftly, he began scaling the side of the building.

Reaching the window he wanted, he deactivated the alarm and picked the lock. Then he slipped through the window and dropped into the gloom of the Compu-Link lab. Like a living shadow, he moved straight for the personal workstation of Roman Sionis.

Batgirl found the address she was looking for on a dark side street and cut the Batblade to a halt. Robin jammed the Redbird's brakes and fishtailed to a stop right next to her. They were facing a vacant lot strewn with ancient rubble and years of weeds.

"So what's this?" Robin asked.

Batgirl allowed herself a brief, bitter smile. "The home address," she said, "listed by Roman Sionis in his personnel file."

"Okay, so there's maybe something weird about your boss," Robin said. "Unless he lives under a rock?"

"I don't think so."

"A broken brick?"

"Uh-uh."

"Basement apartment?"

"Nope."

"Okay, so there's something *definitely* weird about your boss. Now what?"

Batgirl reached down to snap the cap from a small tube attached to the Batblade's frame. She fished out some papers. "So now," she said, unrolling the papers, "we fall back on these records I found in Roman's desk."

Robin seemed surprised. "You stole them?"

Batgirl shook her head. "Photocopied them," she said. "And see here?" She leaned forward to hold the papers in the beam of her cycle's headlamp. Several areas were highlighted. "He authorized three different shipments to an address which matches no client WayneTech has ever dealt with, past or present — and believe me, I checked."

Robin was impressed. He gunned the Redbird's throttle. "So why are we sitting here breathing rubble dust?"

Batman slid down his line, dropped to the pavement, and snapped his grapnel from the gargoyle. Although he had been unable to obtain definite proof in the lab, it was at least possible that Barbara Wilson's suspicions were correct. The young woman was admirably resourceful, if somewhat impetuous.

But now it was time to pursue the lead Gordon had passed on from one of the original smugglers. Since the man was trying to plea-bargain for less prison time, his information could well prove accurate.

The Dark Knight melted into the shadow, coiling his line as he moved swiftly toward the Batmobile waiting in an alley less than a block away.

"Dark Side of the Moon?" Robin said.

"Looks like it used to be a nightclub," Batgirl said, "maybe back when you were shaking your booty in the disco daze."

"Hey, speak for your own booty, girl. That was way before my time."

"All right, all right," Batgirl said. "Let's just get down

with our bad selves and crash this dead party, shall we?"

They had already hidden their cycles under an overpass several blocks away. Now, as carefully and quietly as possible, they pried a splintered sheet of plywood from a boarded-up window of the abandoned club. Batgirl peered into total blackness. There was nothing to see. She slipped inside. Robin followed.

It was almost silent — nothing but the soft stirrings and chitterings of rats and mice, maybe the sound of cobwebs fluttering in the breeze. Batgirl and Robin stood perfectly still, turning their heads from side to side, giving their eyes time to adjust. They seemed to be in a vast empty space. *Probably the main dance floor,* Batgirl decided, *back in the Jurassic Era.* She turned in Robin's direction and softly whispered: "We should've worn our other masks — the ones with the night-vision lenses."

"Now you think of it," he hissed back.

They waited another minute longer. Nothing lunged from the darkness. The ceiling did not collapse. Nor did the floor crack open and swallow them whole. But they still couldn't see a blessed thing. Maybe this really *was* the dark side of the moon.

"Think it's safe," Batgirl whispered again, "to use a light?"

Robin whispered back, "Do it, and we'll know."

So she reached down to her belt and slipped a special

penlite from one of its compartments. She didn't understand how or why, but it was far brighter than any similar flashlight she had ever seen — brighter by a factor of ten, at least. Batman's own design, battle-tested in heavy-duty darkness.

The tightly focused beam swept through nothing but empty space and floating dust. Batgirl slowed its sweep to a crawl and finally, way in the back, it picked out the dull gleam of a doorknob. "There," she whispered. "If there's anyone or anything here, it's behind that door."

She turned toward Robin, angling the light upward to avoid blinding him, and they were immediately surrounded by a thousand dancing flecks of light. They both gaped.

"A mirrored disco ball," Batgirl breathed, almost in disbelief.

"Boogie on," Robin whispered.

They slipped across the vast dance floor toward the gleaming doorknob. It was like crossing a hardwood ocean. Finally Batgirl stationed herself facing the door. Robin flattened against the wall next to it.

"Ready?" Batgirl whispered.

"It's your dance," Robin replied.

Batgirl leaped forward, kicking the door right off its hinges. It banged and bounced and crashed into the smaller room beyond as she hurtled right past it, skidding and tumbling across the floor before rolling back up to her feet. Robin came off the wall and pivoted into the room right behind her.

But they were alone. Batgirl held her stance for another beat, flicking her light into every corner, high and low. It was difficult to identify what was in the room, but nothing moved. She relaxed. "Guess we can finally stop whispering," she said in her loudest voice.

"Yeah." Robin tried the wall switch on a whim and it worked. "How 'bout that," he said. "Let there be light."

"And proof," Batgirl said, "proof at last." She was making a beeline for racks of electronic components arrayed against the back wall. "This is some of the equipment Roman requisitioned — which he *said* he was working on at *home*."

"Hey," Robin said, "here's something even better." He was holding the face of a weeping clown. Several other masks were laid in a row across the workbench next to him.

"Yes!" Batgirl exclaimed. "We nailed it!"

"Slots in the masks are empty," Robin said. "Must be waiting for another shipment of 'mystery chips.' Although they're hardly a mystery anymore, are they?"

"No," Batgirl agreed. "They're mind-control chips." She

had turned back to the component racks and was frowning as she skimmed her eyes across them. "You know," she said, "the really important WayneTech equipment is still missing."

"Like what?" Robin asked.

"Like special amplifiers and converter circuitry that could work in tandem with those mind-control chips."

"So where do you think that stuff is?"

Batgirl didn't answer. She was staring at a telephone on the workbench. She moved to it and pressed the button labeled DISPLAY. A row of numbers filled the LED panel.

Robin leaned his head in. "So what's that?" he asked.

"Last number called," Batgirl replied. She plucked the handset from its cradle. There was a dial tone. She stabbed REDIAL and stuck the handset in Robin's startled face. "Here," she said, "you do the talking. And pretend you're a Black Mask goon. Keep your voice low and rough." She cocked her head close to his, ready to listen in.

"And emotionless," Robin said as they listened to rings at the other end. "Don't forget emotionless. Black Mask goons are *very* big on monotone."

"Shhh." The ringing had stopped.

"Red Arrow Radionics," a weary voice said. "Shipping."

"Uh . . . right, Red Arrow," Robin said in a phony zombie voice. "I'm calling for Black Mask."

"Yeah, yeah, I *told* ya — the shipment's on its way. Driver just called in, matter o' fack. He's on Route 80. Should be hittin' Gotham in about twenty minutes."

Robin didn't know what else to say, so he twisted his head to look past the phone at Batgirl. They were forehead to forehead. Batgirl raised an eyebrow.

"Uh, very good, Red Arrow," Robin vamped. "And just to verify, the driver will be delivering at . . . ?"

"At the address you gave us," the voice snapped gruffly. "Say, who *is* this anyway?"

"Uh . . . sorry, wrong number," Robin blurted. Then he racked the phone as if it had turned into a hot potato.

Batgirl managed to stifle her giggle but not a smirk.

Robin gave her a defiant look. "What?" he demanded.

"Nothing," she said, covering her mouth with a gloved hand. "I just didn't realize you were such a smooth operator, that's all."

"Go ahead and laugh," Robin said, "but *you* try being a zombie." His lower lip was actually thrust out. "It's not that *easy,* you know!"

Batgirl burst out laughing. "Is it harder," she spluttered, "than being a rocket scientist? Or maybe a brain surgeon?" She laughed even harder. "How about a four-star general? A *Boy Wonder?*"

Robin's petulance didn't stand a chance. "All right." He

smiled. "So maybe being a zombie only rates a three on the difficulty scale. Maybe even a minus-ten. Now where does it leave us?"

Batgirl's laughter faded. "Well," she said, "the Red Arrow shipment — whatever it is — could be coming here."

"And on the other glove," Robin said, "it could be going anywhere — some different Black Mask hideout."

Batgirl nodded. "Yeah," she said, "maybe wherever the missing WayneTech equipment is."

Robin's hands started moving as he worked it out. "If the truck's coming off Route 80, then it'll probably take the Coit Causeway right over the Hub," he said. "And by the way, this shipment could be the lead Batman's following tonight . . ."

"In which case," Batgirl said, "he might need our help."

"He certainly needs proof that we can prove ourselves."

"A display of peerless prowess," Batgirl said.

"Efficient and exemplary teamwork," Robin said.

"Initiative without recklessness."

"Piece of cake."

They slapped their palms high.

The Batmobile was running without lights, and the truck driver was still unaware he was being tailed.

Batman had waited opposite the Route 80 exit ramp, just as the smuggler had instructed. And the semitrailer truck had not been difficult to spot, not with giant letters spelling RED ARROW RADIONICS across both sides.

Now the truck was apparently headed for the long elevated span of the Coit Causeway, placing its destination somewhere on the far side of the Hub. Batman kept his distance, hoping the light traffic would thin even further. Right now there were just enough oncoming vehicles to prevent him from overtaking the truck should he wish to make such a move, and his options would narrow even more on the Coit — literally narrow, given the causeway's notoriously cramped lanes. But as long as the truck driver didn't spot him, it wouldn't matter.

Then, just at the foot of the causeway, the truck abruptly veered and righted itself. Batman gave an involuntary snarl as he watched the driver's arm reach from the cab window to adjust the large side mirror. That was it, then: he'd just been spotted in the mirror.

No sense staying back now. He flicked on the Batmobile's powerful headlamps and the truck veered wildly in response. Horns blared. Up ahead, an oncoming car tried to get out of the truck's path but had nowhere to go. It swerved into the guardrail, grinding off a long spray of sparks.

Batman could see the car was out of control and might spin off the rail into his path. He stomped the accelerator and shot ahead to prevent it. There was a long squeal behind him, and then he was forced to jam his own brakes before he ran right up under the semi, more than likely shearing off the Batmobile's roof and quite possibly his own head as well. He watched the Batmobile's front end go under the truck. It would be close. He held the brake and fought the wheel. The truck's bumper grazed the windshield right in front of him.

And then there was separation as the Batmobile continued to slow and the truck struggled up the steep grade of the causeway. Batman faded to a safe distance and simply followed. There was nothing else he could do, not while they were here on the narrow causeway, not without endangering innocent drivers. He had hoped to follow the truck all the way to Black Mask. Now that the truck driver had spotted him, however, he might lead Batman on a merry chase to nowhere, but hardly straight to Black Mask.

He wished there was some way to stop the truck. The oncoming vehicles were still blaring and screeching and skidding into the guardrail. Some rear-ended, and the truck itself had bashed at least three or four others. They were nearing the summit of the causeway's elevation, and it was a long drop to the dark buildings and avenues of the Hub below. Disaster seemed inevitable. If a section of guardrail gave way . . .

The Red Arrow driver was so intent on watching the Batmobile in his mirror that he almost missed the spectacle right up front. There was a long gap in the traffic, and it was the snapping of the capes that finally caught his eye. He looked forward just in time to see two weird motorcycles veer into his lane. Incredibly, they popped wheelies right in his face and kept on coming.

He could have plowed right through them, but instead he panicked. He had never seen anything like this and he simply didn't know what to do, so he did the worst thing possible. He slammed on the brakes, spun the wheel, and jackknifed his semi at the crown of the Coit Causeway.

And, since he was not wearing his seat belt, he also slammed his thick head unconscious.

Batman ejected from the Batmobile, soared through the air, and landed at the rear of the jackknifed truck. All traffic had halted. He wasn't sure why the truck had lost control, but he was more interested in the nature of its cargo. Glad that the danger had passed, he opened the back of the truck and froze.

Inside were a half-dozen masked thugs, all pointing large guns at his head and chest. The sound of bullets jacking into chambers was loud and menacing and unmistakable.

Creeping along the top of the truck, Batgirl and Robin were about a dozen feet short of the rear when they heard the weapons being primed. Batgirl caught sight of Batman and instantly stomped the truck roof as hard as she could. Then she and Robin dived forward to the rear edge as bullets ripped and stitched through the roof behind them.

Together, they flipped over the edge and swung down into the back of the truck, already kicking and batting weapons aside. Then they went to work on the masks.

It was all over in no time, and there was little for Batman to do other than watch.

Robin hunched over a crate deep in the truck as Batgirl dropped down to face the Dark Knight. "The driver's out of it," she said. "Won't be talking for hours."

"Nothing in here but more mind-control chips," Robin reported. "Enough to build the ranks of the False Face Society into a *real* army." He dropped out of the truck to join them. "But still worthless, I assume, as clues to Black Mask's larger scheme."

Batgirl indicated an unmasked thug hanging out of the truck. "And even if we'd left any of these maskers awake," she said, "they'd be just as useless as all the others — brain-blanked stooges."

And having thus assessed and reported the situation, Batgirl and Robin fell silent and stood waiting.

Batman stared at them for a long time. "You did well," he finally said. "Both of you."

It was the opening Batgirl had hoped for, and she rushed to fill it. "We've been thinking," she said quickly. "Instead of seeing us as a 'double responsibility,' why not cut your worry in half now that you have a second partner?" She had actually worked on the line in advance, hoping it would appeal to his sense of cool, rational logic.

But again Batman just stared, his dark mask betraying nothing.

"Aw, come on," Robin said, "at least Batgirl and I can watch each other's back, and that frees *you* up, right?" Then he reached over to slap Batgirl's back, as if presenting this year's new and improved model. "And by the way," he continued proudly, "she was totally right about that weird boss of hers. If he's not Black Mask himself, Roman Sionis is definitely fused to the geek's spine. We found big-time proof all over the place."

Batman turned away, looking out over the guardrail at all the city's lights below. "You did demonstrate teamwork and initiative," he conceded.

"But not too much recklessness?" Robin cracked.

Batgirl kicked his ankle, then extended her fist in front of Batman. "Partners?" she asked.

Robin hopped forward on his good leg and touched his fist to hers. They both waited.

The Batman hesitated . . .

And then made the fists three. *"Partners,"* he said.

On cue, the Bat-Signal blazed upward through the sky until it was stopped by a dark cloud high above the causeway.

"Here's his blackmail demand," Commissioner Gordon said grimly to the three heroes facing him on the roof of police headquarters. He held a finely detailed Chippewa ceremonial mask made from sheets of white birch bark. "It's inscribed on the inner surface: 'fifty million dollars by midnight or I unleash elf to black out and blank the whole city.' Although I don't understand what's so threatening about an elf."

"E.L.F., Commissioner," Batman said. "Extremely low frequency microwaves — the key to the E.D.O.M. and R.H.I.C. technologies I told you about."

Gordon grunted. "Which he uses to control his gang members. And now he's threatening to turn it on all of Gotham. But how he hopes to mask everyone in the city, I don't —"

"He doesn't have to," Batgirl interjected, "not with

the equipment he's stolen, and a twisted application of parallel-linked computer sequencing."

Everyone turned to her. It was clear that she spoke with authority, holding the key to their questions. Even Gordon was now regarding her as a serious equal, searching for his city's salvation somewhere in her masked face. She glanced at Batman and caught his eye. He remained silent, but she could tell he had already figured it out. Master detective that he was, he might even be way ahead of her. Yet he was willing to let her do all the talking and seem like the brilliant one. She could have hugged him — if he weren't so scary, anyway.

She took a breath and began slowly, knowing she had to avoid blowing her other identity as Barbara Wilson. So when she told Gordon about Roman Sionis, she made him seem like a suspect who was under surveillance rather than her boss. "He's made various statements," she said, "about hive minds enslaved to a single master controller. He also raved about parallel linkage of human brains, something he bragged he could accomplish with 'the right kind of radionics and delivery system' — and 'a signal of the proper frequency transmitted into every home.'"

"The ELF frequency," Gordon said. "But what kind of 'delivery system'?"

Batman provided the final piece. "The transmitting tower," he said, "atop the Wyvern Building."

Batgirl looked at him and they both nodded at the same memory — Roman actually showing the notes and blueprints for his master plan to Bruce Wayne, using the proof of his guilt as evidence for his innocence. The man's audacity was astounding.

"Whoa," Robin said. "I'm just getting it now. Really getting it, I mean. The city's main telephone and cable feeds are located at the top of the Wyvern too, aren't they? So if he takes control of that building, he can reach everyone with a radio, television, computer, or phone — which means zombie mush for just about every brain in the city."

"More than that," Batman said. "The power surge from such an ELF feed would blow out every electronic device in the grid — and result in a massive power failure as well."

"A darkness of zombies," Batgirl murmured. "And a nightmare for outside rescue workers."

Gordon looked worried. "Then his 'ELF' really can blank and black us out — unless I can get City Hall to agree to his ransom demand by midnight."

Batgirl shook her head. "I think he'll do it even if you pay, Commissioner. I think he *wants* to do it. Besides, he's got nothing to lose — and a whole city of slaves to gain."

"Then what can we . . . ?"

"We can stop him," Batgirl said. "And we will."

Batman and Robin were already heading for the edge of the roof. "I know we just redeemed ourselves and all," Robin said, "so you may be shocked to learn that we're still not exactly perfect. We, uh . . . we kinda forgot our night lenses, see, and all this talk about blackouts and —"

"Spare sets," Batman said, "in the car." Then he turned to see what was keeping Batgirl.

"If you have just another minute?" Gordon asked.

Batgirl turned back to the Commissioner, who somehow seemed both nervous and grateful. "Frankly," he said, "I really didn't know what to make of you at first."

"I could tell."

"It's just that . . . well, I have a daughter roughly your age. I guess I worry about her too much. And I wasn't sure it was wise of the Batman to take on another partner. I can see now that my doubts were misplaced." He extended his hand.

Batgirl reached out to clasp it. "I shared a few of those doubts myself," she said. "But you're right, Commissioner. They *were* misplaced."

Then she turned and loped across the roof to join her waiting partners. They had less than two hours to pull off something big, maybe even a miracle. If they failed, Gotham would become a city of zombies.

CHAPTER 9
CORNERING DRAGONS

The Wyvern Building rose from Gotham's central skyline like a black splintered sword. Identical dragon gargoyles, glisteningly alien, perched at each of the roof's four corners to keep watch against time. Their ornately jagged wings were spread and extended inward, tips overlapping to encircle the roof itself as well as the towering broadcast spire rising from the roof's center. If they were meant to be the guardians of the Wyvern antenna, they were about to fail.

Attack would come not from the sky, but from within.

The night guard in the main lobby had just begun to doze when the entire world exploded around his head. He jerked awake to find plate glass flying everywhere. One wall of the lobby seemed to be missing, and in its place a strange vehicle was grinding through the wreckage on giant treads. It was an LST, an amphibious troop carrier stolen from the South Port Armory earlier in the evening, and it had just plowed right into the ground-floor lobby of the Wyvern Building.

Mouth agape, the guard watched as the vehicle swerved and quivered to a halt. A wide door levered open from its top and slammed down to become a ramp. Scores of men poured forth, crunching glass underfoot. They were all masked, and every mask was different. They wore tight black outfits and looked like creepy-faced commandos. The night guard thought to reach for his weapon only after they were already swarming him.

Three other guards rushed in from various points throughout the lobby. They too were immediately over-powered.

"Take their weapons," Black Mask commanded. "Then bind their wrists and throw them out of here!" He was standing at the center of the chaos. "This building is ours now," he snarled, "and its power is mine!"

He turned to a man holding a sledgehammer, whose mask made him look like third goon from the bottom on a totem pole. "All right," Black Mask said, "take out the passenger elevators."

The man dragged his sledgehammer all the way across the marble floor. He stopped in front of an electrical access box and smashed it open. Then he stuffed a modest wad of

Plastique explosive inside and backed off twenty paces before thumbing an electronic detonator.

There was a small explosion. All up and down the banks of elevators, indicator lights blinked out.

Black Mask turned back to the LST. Four men masked like apes — chimp, gibbon, baboon, and gorilla — were wheeling a large cart down the ramp. "Careful with that," Black Mask snapped. It was a gleaming assortment of electronic components housed atop a generator mounted to the cart's base. "Get it onto the freight elevator — now."

Then Black Mask turned to the rest of his obediently waiting gang. Behind his ebony mask, he gloated and sneered. Each and every one of these men would fight and die for him, but only because they had no choice. They were nothing but puppets, and he worked the strings to their weak minds with utter contempt. Soon he would sneer at the whole city. "I want ten more men on the freight elevator — and up in the control room — with me and the ape-techs."

Like lemmings, ten masked men counted themselves off and filed toward the freight elevator.

"Then I want three men stationed on every landing in the stairwell," Black Mask continued. "The rest of you will stay here and hold the lobby against whatever may come. And trust me, it will not be a lengthy siege. What remains to be done now is so simple that monkeys could do it."

Then he strode to the freight elevator.

"Going up," he said. "To the top."

The Batblade and the Redbird flanked the Batmobile closely, all three engines idling with quiet power and lights off. They could see the shattered plate glass across the street, and dark shapes milling through the lobby.

"He's already here," Batman said, "and the fuse has been lit. No time to plan. We simply move. I'll create confusion on the way in. Then we hit them hard and fast, and we don't let up until they're all down."

Batgirl and Robin nodded.

"And watch those weapons," Batman added.

The Batmobile peeled across the street with the two motorcycles screeching right behind.

A small bulbed missile shot from a tube above the Batmobile's front bumper. It flashed ahead, streaking into the lobby. There was a muffled *krumph*. A concussion bomb.

The masked gangsters were dazed and staggering when the three vehicles blasted into the lobby. Batgirl and Robin leaped right off their roaring cycles, each hero plowing into a different knot of thugs. Their cycles bowled over others.

The Batmobile was still swerving to a halt when Batman ejected and catapulted right over the LST to land amidst the largest group of Black Mask soldiers. He shot his wrist-grapnel around a Greek oracle's leg and yanked him off his feet. Then Batman spun around on his heels, whipping the man in a circle, beating back a dozen others and making room for the real fight.

In the top-floor control room under the transmitting tower, Black Mask stood like the new lord of a conquered domain, unaware that it had already been invaded. "Jam that freight elevator," he said to one of his thugs. "Make sure it stays right here."

There were three other ways into the control room: one passenger elevator, the stairwell door, and a ceiling hatchway giving access to the roof. Black Mask wasn't worried about any of them. All the passenger elevators had already been blown out of commission, and men were stationed on every stairwell landing all the way up through the entire height of the building, with ten more right here inside the door. And if Police Commissioner Gordon wanted to try the ceiling hatch, let him. The entire city would be enslaved long before any such rooftop operation could be mounted — indeed, long before the midnight deadline.

Black Mask smiled bitterly. It was highly unlikely, of course, that the authorities would ever figure out his ingenious plan. But if they somehow did, he knew, they would have to induce their own deliberate blackout just before the deadline. With his special generator, he would still be able to transmit his ELF signals, so the only way to foil the plan would be by preventing the reception of those signals.

Which was why the deadline had been bogus from the start, along with the ransom demand. Fifty million was peanuts when the city was worth hundreds of billions.

Black Mask turned to his techs. "All right, apes," he said, "start splicing my equipment into the antenna and cable feeds."

Down in the lobby, bodies were sprawled just about everywhere, their masks and guns scattered. Not a single shot had been fired.

Batgirl and Robin watched from a distance as Batman located the only passenger elevator, isolated from the others, that went all the way up to the top-floor control room. He took a mini-explosive from his belt and forced the elevator doors open just enough to jam it between them. Then he ducked around a corner and waited for the small explosion to release the pneumatic catches. When he stepped back out to try the doors, they slid to the sides without resistance.

He turned and looked down a row of other elevators at Batgirl and Robin out in the main lobby. "I'm going up this shaft," he said. "You can try the stairwell — but the minute it becomes too dangerous, back off."

Then he turned away and was swallowed by the blackness of the elevator shaft.

"What do you think?" Batgirl said. "The red one or the green one?"

They were at a breaker panel in a utility room not far from the stairwell.

"Hey, don't be stingy," Robin said. "Snip 'em both."

Batgirl did so.

Robin peeked outside. "One of 'em did the trick," he said. "The stairwell just went dark."

They crossed to the door and paused to listen. Confused voices echoed down the long concrete twist of stairs. "Goons galore," Robin said. "Not gonna be an easy climb."

"Neither is Mount Everest."

"Yeah, so?"

"So," Batgirl said, "nothing else is *worth* the climb." She reached up to click on her night-sight lenses.

Robin did the same. Cool green details resolved from the blackness of the stairwell. "First advantage," he said, "ours."

"Got your earplugs ready?" Batgirl asked.

"Yeah. Their guns are gonna make an incredible racket in there. It's nothing but one long, tall echo chamber."

Batgirl reached for her belt. "Think I'll start with a few flash bombs," she said. "How about you?"

"Probably smoke pellets," Robin replied.

"Ready?"

"Go!"

Batgirl slowly turned the knob, then abruptly shoulder-slammed the door and lunged through with Robin right on her heels. Hurling smoke and flashes and bangs ahead of them, they went up three steps at a time and slammed the first guards down before they knew what was coming.

"Keep going!" Batgirl urged. "Don't give them a chance to brace for us."

They raced up the second flight and Batgirl leg-whipped a man in a volcano demon mask just as he raised his gun. The shot missed by a mile, but even with earplugs they found the explosion nearly deafening as it reverberated up and down the stairwell. Robin elbow-smashed a stylized alligator mask and kicked Richard Nixon flat.

Batgirl shoved Robin's back. "Go, go, *go!*" she urged.

They fought their way up through eleven more landings before they were suddenly pinned down by a hellish hail of gunfire. It had started with a single shot from high above. And then, within seconds, it seemed like there was at least one gunman firing down at them from every landing above, near and far, creating so many muzzle flashes that the darkness became strobe-lit. "And here I thought we'd escaped Disco-land," Robin muttered.

Bullets rocketed and ricocheted everywhere. Cement flinders burst from the walls to sting their chins and cheeks. They tried to make themselves flatter against the wall, tried to shrink themselves to smaller targets.

"Remember how we were supposed to back off," Robin said, "if it became too dangerous?"

"Yeah?"

"Think it's time to back off yet?"

Batgirl gave him a thin, mirthless smile. "Over my reckless body, buster."

"All right, but if we're talking about forward and upward," Robin said, "I can't budge another inch. How 'bout you?"

Batgirl shook her head. "Not without getting shot."

A bullet smacked off the wall and whined past, so close they could feel its hum.

"This situation," Robin said, "is really starting to get on my nerves."

"Mine too."

"So, uh . . . got a plan?"

"Yeah," Batgirl said, "hit 'em where it hurts." Careful to

keep her arm close to her flattened body, she reached for the back of her belt.

"And where would that be?"

"In the ears," she said, slipping a sonic Batarang from the small of her back. She pressed a stud in its side, took a breath, and braced herself. Then she stepped right out to the center of the stairwell and hurled the Batarang straight upward through the muzzle flashes with all the force she could muster. The instant it left her hand, the Batarang began shrieking like a thousand banshees riding berserk bats through a bagpipe regiment. It was an ungodly, keening wail designed to do one thing and one thing only: slice and dice eardrums into utter submission.

The booming, strobing gunfire stuttered to a stop, and the stairwell was again seen through the cool green filters of their night-vision lenses. Strangled cries of pain and confusion came from above. A few guns actually clattered and bounced down past them. Then the sonic Batarang fell back down, still shrieking.

Batgirl and Robin clamped their hands over their ears and waited for it to plummet past.

"All clear," Batgirl said. "How many floors in this building?"

"Thirty-nine, I think."

Batgirl started up the stairs again. "We're not even

halfway to the top," she said. "Better pick up the pace."

Robin rolled his eyes and trudged up the stairs after her.

Outside, police helicopters buzzed around the four dragons of the Wyvern Building, as if challenging them to a sky fight. Powerful searchlights swept the transmitting antenna and roof, but nothing moved, not yet.

Were it not for his night lenses and the penlite clenched in his teeth, Batman would have been climbing through pitch blackness. As it was, the elevator shaft was still gloomy enough to make his progress treacherous at best. He had already hauled himself, hand over hand, up past some twenty floors of the building. And now, finally . . .

He missed his next grip, slipped, and fell through the dark shaft.

More angry with himself than panicked, he slapped his hand out and caught a cable. He slammed against the shaft wall, absorbing as much of the impact as possible with his thickly muscled shoulder. Then he dangled there, catching his breath, holding the cable as it resonated up and down the shaft like a metal whip.

The man in the chimp mask stopped what he was doing. "What was that?"

"What was what?" the man in the baboon mask replied.

"That *twang*."

The baboon scratched his head. "I didn't hear a *twang*."

"Just keep splicing those feeds," Black Mask said. He rose from his chair at the control console and turned toward the sound. Since this was the elevator's upper limit, the anchor housing was right next to the top of the shaft, left exposed for easy repair and maintenance.

"Someone's in that shaft," Black Mask said. "Probably looking for an elevator."

He wrenched a fire ax from the wall. "Let's *send* him one," he said, and began chopping furiously at the cables wrapped around the anchor housing.

It started as a hum high above him, but swiftly became a roar. Batman looked up to see an enlarging square. It was the bottom of the elevator car, plunging straight down at him. It filled the whole shaft. There was no way to evade it, no escape.

Batgirl and Robin decked another three masked thugs and moved onward and upward. They were really feeling it in the legs now, but they were also very near the top, and that fact gave them a real boost. Only a few more landings, a few more battles, and they would be knocking on the control room door.

Not too late, they hoped.

With the cable twisted around one arm and one leg, Batman ripped the grapnel from his wrist launcher and let it drop.

The elevator car was still hurtling down at him. There was little time.

He jammed a missile into the launcher and fired straight up. The missile hit the bottom of the plunging car, and there was a deep, rumbling explosion.

Batman hugged the shaft wall and let the fireball scorch down past him. It stole his breath for a moment and was gone. Then the remains of the elevator car pelted down as bits and chunks of shrapnel. Tightening his grip on the cable, Batman ducked his head and weathered the storm as best he could.

When the last pieces fell past, he was bruised and even bleeding. But nothing would stop him now.

In the control room, the explosion was heard as a dull boom followed by a rattling of the elevator doors. Black Mask whirled in a rage. "Who is *in that shaft?*"

The man in the gorilla mask looked up from his work and cocked his head questioningly. Chimp, gibbon, and baboon all nodded in confirmation.

"Splicing is complete, Black Mask," the gorilla announced. "Access to everyone in Gotham is now possible."

It was a normal night, more or less, throughout the broad avenues and narrow backstreets of Gotham. Citizens did what they usually did. Some listened to radios, some watched TV. Some jabbered or cooed on the phone, and others surfed the Internet.

Only a few read books in total silence.

And all of them, of course, were completely unaware that their brains were in dire jeopardy.

"You're sure it's ready?" Black Mask demanded.

As one, the four ape-masked men nodded.

"Then a new era in broadcasting," he said, "is about to commence." Slowly, he reached toward the master switch . . .

The stairwell door banged open and Batgirl and Robin came swarming in, all flying fists and sweeping feet.

A Batarang sliced unerringly between three masked guards to smack Black Mask's hand away from the switch. He spun to face the intruders, his frozen mask somehow enraged.

Then another explosion blew the doors right off the elevator shaft behind him. He twisted around to see a dark wraith surging through the smoke. It was the Batman.

Black Mask turned and bolted up the few steps to the ceiling hatch. Batman was a swift darkness flowing in pursuit.

The four ape-masked techs simply gaped as Batgirl and Robin began punching and kicking their way through the guards.

Searchlights from the buzzing police choppers illuminated the rooftop confrontation between Batman and Black Mask. With his back against the base of the huge transmitting antenna, Black Mask had nowhere to go as Batman closed in on him.

Black Mask waited until he was certain he could not miss, then pulled a .45 automatic and opened fire at point-blank range. Batman had already dived for the shadows and was now rolling across the roof as Black Mask fired again and again until his weapon was spent.

Then Batman rose to his full height, stepped from the shadow of a dragon, and began closing in again. Black Mask hurled his empty gun, and Batman barely lifted his hand to swat it aside.

Black Mask turned away and began scrambling up the antenna's superstructure, instinctively seeking higher ground.

With all the guards in the control room felled, Batgirl turned to the real danger. "His transceiver equipment," she said. The four ape-masked techs were blocking it.

Batgirl dropped the gorilla and the chimp with a single flying leap-kick. And Robin decked gibbon and baboon with an old-fashioned one-two.

Batgirl moved to the transceiver equipment and frantically began yanking splice cables from its feeds. Robin joined her and kicked the entire wheeled cart onto its side, smashing generator and components alike.

They came out onto the roof in time to see Batman scaling the antenna after Black Mask.

"That computer creep had better watch it," Robin commented, "or he's gonna broadcast *himself* all over the city."

Black Mask couldn't believe he'd come so close, only to be thwarted at the very last second. He hated the dark figure below him, the ruthless and relentless pursuer who had spoiled everything and chased him all the way up here into the high winds at the top of Gotham. It wasn't fair. He had chosen Bruce Wayne and Police Commissioner James Gordon as his opponents, not this supernatural being nipping at his heels. Even worse, he had already outwitted and defeated Wayne and Gordon — both of them — and yet his victory was still being spoiled!

In supreme rage, he thrashed his foot wildly down at his nemesis.

Batman darted back, evading the kick, and Black Mask lost his balance, then his grip.

With a strangled cry, he pitched off the antenna into the start of what would be a long, long fall.

Batgirl had already leaped out onto the intertwined wings of two dragon gargoyles. *"Robin!"* she shouted. *"Anchor me!"*

Robin grabbed her left hand and dug his heels in at the edge of the roof — even as Batgirl used her right arm to hurl a Batline that snagged the plummeting Black Mask at the last second and the very limit of the line.

Robin simply gaped as Batgirl dropped from the dragon wings back to the roof, giving *his* cheek a peck of mock chivalry. "Thanks," she said, "for the slight assist."

Then she hauled up on her line until she had Black Mask back on the roof. He swung at her in rage. She blocked his punch and smashed him with a crunching right cross that shattered his dark mask. The wooden shards fell away to reveal the glazed face of Roman Sionis. She let go and he crumpled. "Yes," she murmured to herself. "Told you so."

Then she stood over the unconscious villain and said more emphatically: "Mr. Sionis, I'd tender my resignation . . . but I suspect you're fired."

"Effective immediately," said a deep voice from above.

She looked up to see Batman dropping down from the antenna. He landed facing her, part of his billowing cape finally settling down to mantle one of her shoulders as well. Then he put a hand on her other shoulder, looked her straight in the eye, and said: "But *your* job is safe — for as long as you want it."

She wished she could stay there like that forever, safe and triumphant and accepted, strong and sure on a high roof within the protective wings of cornering dragons.

EPILOGUE

WAITING DARKNESS

Well," Barbara said, pulling off her mask and making a big show of looking around, "if I'm going to stay in this cave, I think it's time to discuss some changes in decor."

Batman and Robin glared at her. Murderously.

But she was only tweaking them. "Don't worry," she said with a grin. "Your basic Batcave — deep black and grim, gritty gray — is cool with me. At least it can't clash with anything — and besides, I hear *noir* colors will be all the rage this year."

Alfred beamed as he turned to Batman. "No doubt about it, sir. You were indeed right about young Barbara, in every detail."

"Neither of us lost faith in her spirit or abilities," Batman said. "We were both right about her, Alfred."

"Hey, wait a minute," Barbara said. "I thought I just proved you were wrong about me."

Alfred simply smiled and winked. Then he turned sober

and dignified, shooting his cuffs, tugging his vest points, and turning smartly to exit. But he took no more than three steps before pausing to speak as if in afterthought. "By the way," he said, "I shouldn't shed those costumes just yet if I were you. The Bat-Signal is blazing, you see, *again*." Then, having said his piece, the butler resumed his exit.

Batman looked at his partners. "Ready?"

Batgirl and Robin answered in unison: "And then some."

Three gloved fists touched in one-for-all, all-for-one fashion.

And the Batmobile, Batblade, and Redbird roared from the cave, following the Signal's light to whatever darkness awaited.

ABOUT THE AUTHOR

DOUG MOENCH is fast approaching the end of his third decade of writing. His credits include novels, short stories, newspaper feature articles, book/movie/record reviews, magazine copy, dramatic radio and LP records, comic books, syndicated newspaper strips, film screenplays, and teleplays.

In comics, Moench has written for Warren, Skywald, DC Comics, Marvel Comics, Byron Preiss Visual Publications, various underground publishers, Heavy Metal Publications, Eclipse, Kitchen Sink, Dark Horse, Malibu, and others. Although precise records have never been kept, it is very possible that Moench has written more comic book pages than anyone else in history. He is currently writing *Batman,* one of the oldest ongoing comic book titles in the business. Characters and series of his own creation or cocreation include *Schreck, Freaks, Spook, Deathlok, Moon Knight, Weirdworld, Electric Warrior, Aztec Ace, Six from Sirius, Slash Maraud, Lords of the Ultra-Realm, Coldblood,* and *Xenobrood.* Moench has also worked on *Master of Kung Fu, King Conan, Doc Savage, Man-Wolf, Planet of the Apes, Godzilla, Frankenstein, Thor, Fantastic Four, Werewolf by Night, Iron Fist, The Rampaging Hulk, The Inhumans, Captain Marvel, Shogun Warriors, Tales of the Zombie, Dracula Lives!, Sherlock Holmes, Man-Gods from Beyond the Stars, Merlin, Kull, Sgt. Rock, House of Mystery, House of Secrets, Arion, World's Finest, the Wanderers, C.O.P.S. Detective Comics, Spectre, Batman: Legends of The Dark Knight, Mister Miracle, Rune, Batman,* and *Catwoman.* Moench's graphic novels and collections include *Six from Sirius, More Than Human, Legends of the Dark Knight: Prey, Sandkings, Batman & Dracula: Red Rain, Batman: Dark Joker — The Wild, Batman: Bloodstorm, Batman: Knightfall, James Bond: Serpent's Tooth, Batman-Spawn: War Devil, Batman: Brotherhood of the Bat,* and *The Big Book of Conspiracies,* among others.

Moench and his works have been honored many times — with the Eagle, World Fantasy, Diamond Gemstone, Inkpot, Eisner, and other awards — and he was nominated for a Chicago Newspaper Guild Award in 1972. *Time* magazine listed *The New Adventures of Mighty Mouse,* for which Moench was story editor and head writer, as one of the Ten Best TV Shows of 1987, while the *Wall Street Journal* named it the best.

Born in 1948, Moench lived in Chicago until the age of twenty-five, when he moved to Manhattan for two years. He has also lived briefly in Scotland and Los Angeles. He and his wife, Debra, have resided in Bucks County, Pennsylvania, since 1975. They have one son, Derek, and a golden retriever named Rusty.